MCCURDY INVESTIGATIONS

SH*TS AND GIGGLES INC.

MELVIN DEFOREST

McCurdy Investigations
Copyright © 2024 by Melvin Deforest.

All rights reserved. No part of this publication may be reproduced, distributed, or transmitted in any form or by any means, including photocopying, recording, or other electronic or mechanical methods, without the written consent of the publisher. The only exceptions are for brief quotations included in critical reviews and other noncommercial uses permitted by copyright law.

MILTON & HUGO L.L.C.
4407 Park Ave., Suite 5
Union City, NJ 07087, USA

Website: *www.miltonandhugo.com*
Hotline: *1- 888-778-0033*
Email: *info@miltonandhugo.com*

Ordering Information:
Quantity sales. Special discounts are granted to corporations, associations, and other organizations. For more information on these discounts, please reach out to the publisher using the contact information provided above.

Library of Congress Control Number:	2024924103
ISBN-13: 979-8-89285-381-1	[Paperback Edition]
979-8-89285-382-8	[Hardback Edition]
979-8-89285-383-5	[Digital Edition]

Rev. date:10/29/2024

CHAPTER

1

My father once told me that the day you stop learning is the day you start dying. An interesting concept that I am sure has some merit despite the difficulties of establishing it as a scientific fact. He also noted that my historical learning pattern indicated I could live for a very, very, long time. With a stunted ability to learn anything other than via the school of hard knocks, I could conceivably live forever provided my liver doesn't turn into a hockey puck from over exposure to the vile sailor swill marketed by numerous companies with various appealing names and colors designed to disguise its true identity. Rum. "Pirate piss", my significant other had called it when referencing my affinity for it. She had referenced it multiple times in the note she lovingly attached to my luggage that she had deposited haphazardly on the lawn when evicting me for the third, and I suspect, the final time.

I had wallowed in despair for a moment, however, that seemed to be going nowhere, so logic dictated that I get over it and move on. While loading my luggage it occurred to me that she had some irritating habits of her own, not the least of which was referring to my investigations business as "shits and giggles incorporated", as well as referring to my esteemed colleague Oliver Barnett as a funny colored Shrek. I did concur, with Olly, my sometimes partner and assistant that she did have a very nice ass even though she may be a bit light on the top end. The nice ass would be sorely missed as would the warm bed and a home with utilities paid. On this occasion I would defer to the often-stated public opinion, as well as popular theory among friends and acquaintances, that I was just a world class asshole, and therefore, I accepted the majority of the responsibility for the relationship breakdown. Thus justified, responsibility duly accepted, I also deferred to logic and moved on.

The eviction was two days ago, which was just one of the reasons I was waking up in my office today suffering a hangover from hell, courtesy the forementioned pirate piss. My "office" being a converted apartment above a Chinese food restaurant. By converted I mean added a desk, some file cabinets, and the recent required addition of a used hide-a bed.

The other not insignificant reason was a temporary cash flow problem resulting from the untimely demise of McCurdy Investigation Inc.'s most recent, and only paying client, in a hail of bullets graciously provided by the local S.W.A.T. team before he could pay up his account. A reasonably substantial sum, now uncollectable, which would have afforded me better accommodations and at least a mediocre quality of pirate piss.

The said client had loaded his shotgun and stormed the office building where his unfaithful wife was employed. To his dismay, she was absent. Having fired off several rounds already, it was bit late in the game to say "ok, I'll come back another time", so, he made the irrevocable decision to take some of her co-workers hostage and await her arrival.

His postal episode was a reaction to viewing some photographs of his wife in several compromising positions with one particular co-worker, also not present, to serve as an outlet for the said client's frustration.

The pictures were provided courtesy of McCurdy Investigations. The gentlemen, a religious man whom I had assumed would take my professional advice and leave vengeance to the Lord, must have had limited capacity in the patience department. He promised to do so, and may have heeded my advice, and simply had just chosen to move the Lord and his wife's introduction forward a few years. No one will ever know for sure, thank you SWAT.

A miscalculation of the gentlemen's mental stability on my part started a chain reaction of events with disastrous consequences which inevitably lead to the premature death of a usually law-abiding citizen, along with the demise of my bank account.

Perhaps I should not have been so thorough in my investigation, but I believe in giving my clients their money's worth.

I avenged the death of my bank account by killing a bottle of the forementioned sailor's swill.

I learned three things.

Number one, clients cannot write checks when they are dead.

Number two, in marital investigations, demand advance payment.

Number three, learning curves can be costly. Following the philosophy of learning increasing life expectancy, I am not convinced my life expectancy was increased by an equal value to that deducted from my income.

It is what it is and I had, however unintentionally, acquired enough new knowledge to give me a couple of days grace before I start the dying process.

I dragged my carcass off the sofa and made my way to the washroom. I looked much like I felt. A sack of crap does not adequately describe either state. I needed a haircut and had too many wrinkles for my forty-five years. The bloodshot eyes served as a visual aid to any observers that I had seriously exceeded my body's capacity for pirate piss, a tolerance level I have not yet fully established, despite years of intensive study.

I had installed a shower in my office washroom the last time I found myself evicted from my love life and was just completing the process of re-humanizing myself when my cell phone vibrated and quacked like a duck. The caller Id notification informed me it was Oliver. As mentioned earlier, McCurdy Investigations Inc. employee roster consisted of myself, and when I could afford it, an assistant named Oliver Bartholomew Barnett.

"Morning boss" he said.

His accent was as unrecognizable as his heritage. Either could be changed to suit the occasion. Genetics provided the appearance of a Mongolian-Oriental-Hispanic-Caucasian-African American, and the ability to assume any accent was a survival talent acquired growing up between an army base in Korea and the gutters of any and every town in North America. A little time in Montreal even added some French to his vocabulary, or, at least enough of the accent to impress the ladies.

"It is morning," I agreed.

Olli only called me boss to ingratiate himself when he wanted something, and I knew this time what it was.

"Do you think I could get paid boss?'

I was prepared for the question. A good offence beats a good defense every time.

"I wish we both could both get paid Olli, but the SWAT guys shot our paycheck. You work on a twenty percent commission basis and twenty percent of the nothing I got paid is still nothing. If that makes you mad, think about this. The twenty percent of nothing you got screwed over for is not as big as the eighty percent of nothing I got screwed out of, so I have a right to be more pissed than you."

There was a pause on the line while Olli lost his temper. It takes him a minute to heat up and I expected him to do a little venting. I was right. With no reasonable argument on the financial arrangement or the prospect of getting paid, he changed the topic slightly to attack the financial arrangement itself.

"I don't like that twenty percent arrangement Mister M." My name is Melvin. He only called me Mister M when he was pissed at me. He called me Mister M often. "How come you get eighty percent and I only get twenty percent. People shoot at me too"

He wasn't done but I interrupted him.

"We've been through this before Olli. It is my office, my car, and my gun. Twenty percent for the office, twenty percent for the car, and twenty percent for the gun. That leaves twenty percent each for you and me."

Olli stuttered a bit, then raised his voice a decibel or two.

"Twenty percent for that little gun. That's too much…"

"Hang on Olli "I cut him off again.

From where I was standing, I could see the stairway leading up to my second-floor office, and the lady coming up those stairs looked like a million bucks. Stunningly gorgeous would be an understatement. The shiny back Mercedes, she had climbed out of and the apparel she was wearing said she had the bank account to go with her looks.

"Oliver" I shouted into the phone interrupting his rant, "I believe our next payday may be at the door. Bring our gun and come to the office. If I am hallucinating and there is not a stunningly gorgeous lady in the office when you get here … shoot me"

There was a moment's silence on the line. "OK, just make sure you get some money, or I'll shoot you when I get there anyway." He hung up the phone more vigorously than was necessary.

I quickly tossed the blanket off my couch to a hidden position behind it, grabbed a file folder and was sitting at my desk as though I were in deep concentration when she walked in. I waited a few seconds before looking up. First impressions are very important, and I was very impressed. The lady, maybe not so much impressed by me or my office. She was in the upper half of her twenties or very early thirties, five- foot- eight, one hundred-twenty pounds, blond hair, and intelligent blue eyes. There was a vulnerable innocence about her that fueled men's protective instincts. Especially old school fools like me. It just made me want to smack anyone that might do harm to such an obviously beautiful soul assuming her soul was as beautiful as the exterior. She hesitated a moment upon entering to appraise my luxury office facilities. She stopped with the door still open and her hand on the doorknob prepared to make a hasty retreat. Her expression confirmed she was not nearly as impressed by me, or the office, as I was with her.

"Excuse me," I said. "Just going through some resumes. My secretary is on maternity leave."

Not exactly a lie. The last girl to work here has had four children since she left.

I stood, offered my hand, and introduced myself.

After a moment's hesitation and a cursory look to confirm it was clean, she weakly shook my hand "My name is Susan Harcourt" she replied as though I should know the name.

I tried to summon forth where I had heard it before from the glop of porridge that was my brain.

"Dustin Harcourt's wife" she offered, noting my confusion.

The name filtered through the smog in my brain. Dustin Harcourt had a reputation for living the high life. Fast cars, faster women. Wild parties. Rumor was his money came from shady real-estate deals, and possibly some equally shady prostitution and drug dealing. Living just on the edge of the law. Or staying just ahead of it. Not the kind of person I would have pictured to be consorting with this lady's intelligent blue eyes, her assumed beautiful soul and fantastic everything else.

"I see, and what brings you here today?" I queried.

There were plenty of larger firms up town whose expertise people with her kind of money could buy.

She hesitated and stared at the floor wringing her hands together, a sign of shyness, tempered with nervousness. I guessed she was either guilty of something or embarrassed. Either way it told me she was not a practiced liar.

I pushed some magazines off a chair and slid it toward her. "Sit, please" I offered noting her discomfort and interrupting any thoughts she was having about bolting out the door.

She sat in the offered chair, giving it a quick brush with her hand to clear any dust the magazines had left behind. She paused, and spoke slowly, choosing her words.

"I was raised on a farm in the Midwest Mr. McCurdy. I was working as a dental assistant in a small town. I met Dustin Harcourt about 5 months ago. He had chipped a tooth while passing through our little community. After his tooth was repaired, he asked me to dinner. He was very persistent. He stayed in our town for a few days during which time we became well acquainted." She paused and cleared her throat to cover the embarrassment. "Very well acquainted". I am not the morality police. I thought, lucky bastard but kept my mouth shut and waited for her to continue. She took a deep breath, looking down at her hands in her lap, and began again.

"When he left, I thought I would never see him again, however, he returned about a week later. I have never considered myself impulsive but to be brief, after what you would call a whirlwind romance, we were married. That was three months ago. The glamour and glitter, the yachts, the swimming pools, and Mercedes cars may have overwhelmed me. And his charming British accent may have had something to do with it. These expensive clothes, beauty salons, and manicures are all new to me."

She paused, took a deep breath.

I maintained my professional listeners look.

"A few days ago, my husband's car was found at the bottom of a cliff off Compton Road smashed on the rocks. An anonymous caller spotted it at low tide and informed the police. His body has not been found."

I gave that a moment to sink in. My porridge brain was starting to recall hearing of the said incident.

"And he is presumed dead?" I prodded.

She lowered her eyes again.

"The police say there was a small amount of blood in the car and that the tide probably washed his body out to sea."

I tried to sound sympathetic. "That's very possible Mrs. Harcourt. A lot of bodies have been lost to the sea." I neglected to mention that a substantial portion of those bodies who vanished may have been involved in some nefarious activities and were helped overboard with weights attached designed to ensure the bodies were lost at sea.

"The insurance company" she blurted, and then stopped.

Regaining her composure, she began again.

"My husband's legal counsel, Jessica Baird, informs me that my husband had a ten- million-dollar life insurance policy on himself."

I broke the pencil I was taking notes with. The average guy could not afford the premiums on that kind of insurance policy.

She glanced up long enough to let me know that she had noticed the broken pencil.

The synapses in my brain began snapping amid the drum roll left over from the rum. Life insurance was like betting you were going to die and paying those sorts of premiums suggested the buyer may have had some insight into their future that did not come from a crystal ball. A little like betting on horses. Easy if you knew how the race was going to end ahead of time. It is very seldom that healthy people know when they are going to die. More often someone else may know they were going to die when they picked up the gun and went hunting for them, but they didn't call up and say, "Uh hey, maybe you should pay up your life insurance."

Ms. Harcourt interrupted my reverie.

"I'm the sole heir." She added matter-of-factly.

That pushed the synapse voltage in my brain up to melt down. I was glad I had broken the pencil with the earlier revelation. I may have swallowed my tongue. I am as not sure, but for whatever reason, it became temporarily non-functional.

A Midwest farm girl dental assistant pulling in maybe five hundred bucks a week meets high rolling Romeo party guy. Three months later he is dead, and she owns the few million he is already worth, plus ten million dollars insurance. Synapses are firing like Uzi's and all they can come up with is "something is wrong with this picture" but fortunately, the often-faulty check valve between my brain and my tongue was working, and I did not say it out loud. Maybe I could thank my temporarily dysfunctional tongue. I was also thinking this would make the sole heir a most obvious prime suspect and what possible scenario would validate my first impression turned conclusion that this lady with the beautiful soul was a candidate for sainthood and incapable of anything so nefarious as a murder plot.

High rolling city boys take advantage of small-town girls. Not the other way around. I did another quick appraisal to re-evaluate that look of innocence. It was still there.

"Do you find it warm in here?" I asked, getting up to open a window. Suddenly I needed more oxygen to my brain.

"No" she replied, matter-of-factly, and continued. "The insurance company suspects I may have had something to do with his disappearance. They are investigating."

She was talking quickly, trying to get it all on the table. I was struggling to open a window that had been painted shut for sixty years.

"Ms. Harcourt, ten million dollars is a substantial amount of insurance. I can appreciate the insurance company wanting to be thorough. When was this policy taken out?"

I had regained control of my tongue, but my senses were still agreeing with the insurance company. Something is seriously wrong with this picture.

"A few days after we were married. I knew nothing of it until recently. I became angry when he suggested life insurance for us both during our honeymoon and he never brought the subject up again.

A small corner of my brain questioned why life insurance would be a good topic of conversation during a honeymoon, but my check valve was still working, and I kept my mouth shut while my porridge brain analyzed this information.

It just keeps getting better was about all my brain's in-depth analysis came up with.

Guys like Dustin Harcourt did not have a soul, much less a conscience. Why would he insure himself for ten million bucks? I had been wrong about people before but….

Ms. Harcourt went on. "It is not so much about the money, I don't care about that, but there's more Mr. McCurdy."

Oh great, just what we need is more, I thought, as if it was not already enough, lets add to it.

She reached into her purse and brought out an envelope.

I gave up on opening the window and sat down, taking it from her hand as I did.

"A man approached me in a restaurant yesterday and gave me this" she continued.

I took the letter from her hand and opened the envelope removing a typed note.

It read:

Condolences on the loss of your husband.

He owed us 2 million dollars.

Have it ready in cash, within 3 days

We will contact you.

It had no address or no name. It did not need one. It was rubber stamped at the bottom with a snake coiled around a revolver. I had seen it a couple of times tattooed on corpses down at the morgue. It was the mark of a consortium of drug runners, thieves, and murderers, supposedly with connections in the Middle East and Asia. They called themselves Jackals, which did not sound very Middle Eastern to me. Personally, I thought they were just good old born and bred North American vermin. Regardless, they were a nasty bunch. My instincts had been right about Dustin Harcourt. No conscience and no soul fit right in with these guys. How in hell did Ms. beautiful soul with the beautiful exterior and everything else get involved with these people?

This tidbit of information served to quash the life out of any illusions I had about making a fast buck fishing this lady's husband out of the ocean without getting shot at. My easy buck aspirations went out the window and the tiny portion of my brain dedicated to logic was having second thoughts about getting involved.

"Mrs. Harcourt, have you gone to the police with this note?"

She shook her head in the negative and spoke quietly.

"No. Jessica advised me not to. She explained to me who these people were. She said involving the police would only make them angry and they might go after my family as well as myself. I don't want to put my family in any danger."

There was more hesitation and hand wringing.

"And she also mentioned that if they were involved with Dustin's disappearance the insurance company may not pay. Jessica has been so wonderful. I don't know many people here."

She paused while I pondered the insurance part. Good point. Ten million good points.

"Mr. McCurdy, I swear I didn't know, and still do not believe Dustin was involved with these people."

She was either telling the truth or she was the best liar I had ever met, and I have met some very good ones in addition to being an accomplished fibber myself. It explained what she was doing in my office instead of one of the larger corporate firms downtown. For ten million bucks Mother Theresa could keep a secret from the insurance people, and this farmer's daughter had come to the right place if she was looking to buy someone's integrity.

"When did you get this?" I asked.

"Yesterday"

"So that means we have at most two days before they get back to you."

"I'm scared Mr. McCurdy. I simply don't know what to do. Will you help me?"

I could have, should have, and would have, said no to the money had my lips been capable of forming the word. Good sense from that minimalistic logic part of my brain told me to say no.

It might have been the protective instincts in me but, in all likelihood, it was the potential for a decent retainer that got my tongue moving again and said, "Of course, we will do what we can Mrs. Harcourt."

Greed and lack of living accommodations tends to confound my decision-making abilities.

"Thank you" she exhaled with relief.

"We have two days or less before the bad boys come knocking so I'd like to discuss the case with my associate, Oliver Barnett. He should have been here by now. We will contact you early tomorrow morning. Do you have access to two million dollars Mrs. Harcourt?

"I don't know" she replied. "Jessica handles all the finances."

"OK, we can handle that tomorrow as well. Perhaps you could have her meet with us in the morning."

"Of course, I'll arrange a time when speaking with her today" she replied.

I cleared my throat. "Uh, just one more thing Mrs. Harcourt. We will of course require a small retainer.

"Yes of course. Jessica had told me there would be. She highly recommended you. She gave me this to give to you." She passed an envelope across the table. "And please, call me Susan" she said.

I was staring at the ten grand in the envelope. I don't believe my tongue was hanging out, but I may have been wrong.

She stood and offered another envelope. There is more???, I hesitated when taking the envelope. "No worries, this contains my address and all my contact information. Good day then Mr. McCurdy, we will speak again in the morning. I will discuss with Jessica and will let you know when she can be available"

"Call me Melvin" I shook her hand and enjoyed watching her walk out.

Highly recommended by Jessica Baird huh? Who was hell was Jessica Baird, and where the hell did, she know me from, much less know me well enough to highly recommend my services? Was she really as wonderful as Susan Harcourt thought she was?

CHAPTER

2

Oliver was late owing to his mode of transportation. Ms. Harcourt was gone, and Olli had drawn our gun preparing to shoot my hallucination, and me, when I stuffed the twenty percent in his hand. I should be more careful with Olli's instruction. He was quite capable of carrying them out. Especially after a five-mile walk.

"Fifteen hundred bucks up front Oliver and plenty more where that came from." Ok, so my math skills are not that great.

Olly was holding the money in one hand and counting it with the other one still holding the gun.

"What about last week?" he asked.

"You enjoyed taking those pictures anyway Olli. Front row seats to an amateur porn show. Most people would have paid to be in your shoes. Write it off as the price of experience. And next time use a little discretion. Your over-zealous picture taking was at least partially responsible for driving the guy to the brink. Some of those pictures I swear you must have been in the same room. How the hell you do that Olli?"

He ignored my question.

"I guess maybe you're right," he said, holstering his gun and tucking the bills in his wallet. Amazing how a handful of cash can improve someone's disposition.

"Too bad he had to go and get shot. Damn trigger-happy SWAT guys"

He put the gun in his pocket and sat across from me. "You think I could get a date with our now deceased client's widow? She's very talented. Flexible and kind of cute."

"The depths of your depravity never cease to amaze me Oliver, however, we have work to do so get your mind out of the gutter."

"Ok Melvin, but the last time I got paid up front for a job, I got shot down and in the back."

He paused for effect. "Square in the ass."

"From a small shotgun and you were out of range Olli. A little quicker on your feet and you would not have been hit at all. Don't be so dramatic."

"A little quicker on my feet and I would have been running ahead of you and you would have got it in the ass, and your right, I wouldn't have been hit at all. You never even said thanks."

"Thank you for blocking buckshot with your ass Oliver, now can we get on with it. Time is not on our side with this one."

"Still the odd pellet surfaces," he grumbled.

I gave him a rundown on the case trying to make it sound like a piece of cake and it was going rather well until I mentioned the possible Jackal connection.

"The Jackals" he spit it out. "Them fuckers kill their own kin for pleasure. Don't you be handing me no shit about some innocent little farm girl." He was in self-preservation mode indicating he had a tiny portion of logic hidden away in his head as well. Getting laid he was French or Latin, getting mad, he was Italian, getting drunk, he was Caucasian /

Irish, When he got worried they all merged into the true Oliver.

"If she owes the Jackals 2 million bucks she doesn't have enough ass to pay them back I don't care what she looks like" She is likely to die real bad an I don't want to be dead with her for no fifteen hundred bucks"

"Calm down and don't get your panties in a bunch Oli. As I see it, all McCurdy Inc has to do here, is to be the go between. Ms. Harcourt rounds up two million bucks, we deliver it to the bad guys to get them out of the picture. Then, we come up with Mr. Harcourt's body or at least conclusive proof that he is dead. This may require swearing an affidavit using our innovative imaginations and ingenuity stating how we have confirmed his death and the circumstances of this accidental death. Ms. Harcourt picks up her ten million bucks and of course she is so eternally grateful that we have such good imaginations that she gives us at least one of those millions to ensure that our memories stay intact. You and I move to Mexico and buy a nice bar on a nice beach where nobody shoots at our Asses anymore."

Oliver was pondering. Probably doing a risk assessment.

"Senoritas on the beach Olli. No guns. Do you know how much tequila you can buy with twenty percent of a million bucks?"

"Ok, Ok, he finally said. "I'm in, but I want paid every week up front."

"Deal" I said, before he thought of asking for a percentage increase.

He hesitated a bit longer before offering his hand. "Deal" he said, and we shook hands.

"So, Mr. Hotshot detective Melvin McCurdy, how does shits and giggles incorporated proceed from here?"

I ignored the little jab aimed at my relationship failures. It was time to get down to business.

"I'd like to have a look at the car Mr. Harcourt went for the swan dive in. I have immense faith in the local constabulary, but I would like to see for myself if anything looks suspicious. I have known them to miss small things, like bullet holes in the driver's door, especially when the bullets came from one of their service revolvers. If there is blood in the car, I expect Mr. Harcourt would probably be the rightful owner and that could be proven by DNA testing. If there happens to be five quarts of it, that will mean, Mr. Harcourt had none left and therefore must be dead. You never know what you'll find until you look."

The Prospect of Mexican beaches and babes had captured Olly's attention. He was pumped and ready for action. One of the reasons I kept him as a partner, despite his minor deficiencies in the personality department, was his tenacity. Once he got his teeth into a case, he was like a pit bull. Never quit. At the moment, he was pacing the office, shuffling through the cabinets.

"Got any bullets for this gun?" he asked. "Used most of mine this morning."

"This morning. What in hell were you shooting at this morning?"

"The neighbor's cat woke me up" he stated as though that explained it all.

"Jesus Christ Olli," I said. "You live in the city. What were you shooting at, the cat or the neighbor?"

"The cat of course. The neighbor never woke me up. There was no reason to shoot her."

He gave me a quizzical look, like I should have understood the logic of that without being told.

"And nobody notices a little gun fire in the part of town I live in," he added.

I pulled a box of thirty-eights from my desk drawer and tossed them to him.

"What are we waiting for?" he asked. "Mexico awaits my charms. You want to look at the car, let us go look at the car."

"Actually Oliver, we are kind of pressed for time so I thought while I go look at the car, I would drop you off down on the strip and you could do a little socializing. Check out a few of the bars and use some of that infinite charm before you take it all to Mexico. See what you can find out about a relationship between the Jackals and Mr. Dustin Harcourt."

"You mean go down and piss off some jackals," he said without enthusiasm.

"Not at all Oliver. The Jackals run the prostitution and drug trade in this neighborhood and if I am right about Dustin Harcourt, he was involved in both. Buy the ladies a few drinks. Make conversation. Do what your good at. See if you can find out anything that will get us to Mexico a little sooner."

"You're the boss," he said, and holstered his gun.

CHAPTER

3

I had dropped Olli' off at one of the classier joints on the strip, promising to return in two hours, and proceeded over to the DMO where the lady was about as helpful as a unionized tarantula when I inquired as to the location of Dustin Harcourt's vehicle. Susan Harcourt was unsure where they had towed it too, and I was already on the "do not help this bastard let him die list" with the boys in blue. A google search of car impounds returned 575,000 results which was 574,995 more results than I could hope to get to in 2 hours. Consequently, I found myself driving to junk yards, impounds, and auto wreckers listed in the yellow pages of the phone book I had stolen after first finding a pay phone, and secondly finding a pay phone where someone hadn't already stolen the phone book.

I had managed to locate the car in a local impound and was inspecting it with one eye on the pair of Doberman pinchers watching me with a mean, hungry look on their chops. I picked up a short piece of pipe and held it over my shoulder so they understood what was in store for them should they decide to make me their next meal. I was not the kind of person to be eaten without putting up a fight.

The car was a Mercedes very similar to the one Ms. Harcourt arrived at my office in. Possibly purchased as his and hers wedding gifts.

Any blood there may have been had washed away save for a smudge on the headrest that I assumed was the blood the cops had referred to. Far short of the required amount to confirm death of a squirrel much less the carnage I had been hoping for. Not likely enough, or deteriorated too much from being in the salt water for a DNA test.

There were no bullet holes in the body of the car. All of window the glass was missing but was of little concern. When a bullet went through glass and then through someone's head it usually left behind evidence in the form of bone and brain splatter of which there were none.

The cruise control switch was set in the off position which would have been unusual for someone on a coastal road ten miles from the nearest stop but proved nothing. Some people just did not use it. Some people, like myself, if their car had it which in my case it did not.

The four doors were closed. The gear shifter was in the neutral position but may have been placed there by the tow truck operator while loading it. Rear and passenger doors were locked, the driver's door unlocked which was unusual considering the power door locks on a Mercedes lock automatically seconds after the gearshift is placed in drive. Again, it may not be the position it was in when it landed. Still, if someone were to have jumped from the vehicle, it is highly unlikely they would have taken the time to close the door after exiting a vehicle headed over an embankment. For exactly ten million reasons, Dustin Harcourt needed to be in the vehicle accidentally going over the cliff, dying on impact, floating out to sea, and becoming the main course of a passing great white shark before being nibbled clean by other sea scavengers. It was becoming apparent that much ingenuity and imagination would be required to come up with conclusive proof of Harcourt's accidental demise.

The junkyard owner was rushing me. This car was next on the assembly line for the crusher, which was rather curious in my books. Late model Mercedes normally has some value in parting out, regardless the condition of the car body, and save for the roof being squashed flat to the main body, this car was not in as bad a shape as the Chevy Impala I was currently driving. I was of the assumption the vehicle should have been evidence and would be the possession of the law enforcement team charged with investigating the circumstances involved in the car, and Mr. Harcourt's demise. When I inquired as to who had instructed the car be crushed, I was diplomatically informed that it was none of my business. The dogs growled less diplomatically.

One thing I was certain of. If Dustin Harcourt floated out of this car and out to sea, he was less than three inches thick. To sustain this type of damage, the car had to have done an in-flight one-eighty-degree roll, and then a vertical drop flat on its roof. The grill and bumper were quite intact. The largest opening exiting the driver's compartment was less than four inches. Houdini would still have been in the vehicle. It was highly unlikely I could convince an insurance company that Dustin Harcourt was less than 3 inches thick, or that he had exited the vehicle in mid-flight, closed the cars door behind him, then died on impact and floated away.

Dustin Harcourt was more than likely dead, but he was not in this car when it went over the cliff.

Shame to waste a nice car like that.

CHAPTER

4

The promised two hours had turned into three and a half by the time I made it back to the strip to retrieve Olly. His cell phone went directly to voice mail, not uncommon for Olli. He was not fond of interruptions when his charm was turned on high. With a three-hour head start in the clubs, Oliver can be hard to find so I now found myself hopping from sleaze bar to sleaze bar socializing with the very same crowd of "cut your throat for a buck" quality citizens I thought I had so cunningly pawned off on Oliver.

I was about to give up, wait a day or two and start checking the obituaries so I could claim his sorry ass when the door of the quaint establishment I was approaching exploded off its hinges, and Oliver skidded to a face first stop in the parking lot. Two gentlemen who had obviously assisted him through the doorway followed behind. They were quite possibly twins. Three hundred pounds each, not counting the five-pound belt buckles, half bald, long greasy hair, big biceps, bigger bellies, very small wife beater T shirts, and tattoos at least equal to the exposed skin on their bodies. They were easily distinguishable from each other when they smiled though, which they were doing much of. One of them had no teeth and the other one had one large crooked brown tooth.

Nice to see people who enjoyed their work and these gentlemen were enjoying theirs, that is to say, they were enjoying the working over they were giving Olliver.

Mr. One tooth casually walked over and booted Olly in the mid-section hard enough to lift him a off the ground and roll him onto his back.

"Hey," I said, "That's no way to treat a guest."

Mr. No tooth spit his tobacco on the ground and snarled, "Keep moving buddy unless you want to be enjoying some of the same"

"Sorry friend," I said gesturing palms up. "I don't want any trouble."

He glared at me as I walked past the trio and into the bar. I felt kind of bad about leaving Olli to fend for himself, however jumping into the mix would only have served to get me pummeled, and one of us had to stay in presentable shape.

The waitress behind the bar may have been a sister to the Bobbsey twins outside. She was of similar size and build. I would guess she was probably younger. Her mouth was still full of decayed teeth.

"Excuse me madam," I said. "What is the cheapest wine you have by the bottle?"

She studied the liquor menu for a minute. "I guess that would be Corona red. Four bucks for a half gallon."

"I'll take two please," I smiled.

She came back with the wine and her most charming smile. "There you go sir"

"Thank you dear," I smiled back and passed her a ten. "Keep the change"

Oliver had gained some ground when I got back out the door. He had gotten his arms wrapped around One tooth's leg and sunk his teeth into the calf muscle. One tooth was hollering "Get him off" and No tooth was booting Oliver's kidneys. Ouch, that has to hurt like a bitch, I thought, as I strolled up behind No tooth.

Corona red comes in a good thick glass bottle. Ideal for the purpose I had in mind. I took aim on the bald spot on the back of No tooth's head so as not to cushion the blow with any hair, and used bottle number one. It had the desired effect. The bottle smashed, no tooth crumpled to his knees and slumped forward over Oliver's legs, the red wine mixing with the greasy hair.

"Shit" one tooth was screaming as he turned towards me, when bottle number two arrived at its destination. Its target, the one remaining tooth in his head. The bottle shattered leaving bits of glass embedded in the chin and lips, and forever relieving one tooth of any dental fees for his last remaining tooth. He tilted backwards and collapsed with Olli still gnawing on his leg.

"Grrnnk" Olli said, the fat leg still in his teeth.

"Jesus Christ Olli, you have to work on your interpersonal skills. Learn to get along with people."

"Son-of-a-bitch" Olliver groaned after letting go of the leg in his mouth, and struggling to get too his feet.

"Son-of-a-bitch," he said a little louder, holding onto his mid- section in pain.

I was still holding the pistol grip style necks of the two bottles. "That was very good year." I tossed them aside.

"Son-of a-bitch" seemed to be Olli's entire vocabulary. He kept loudly repeating it each time he kicked the unconscious, used to be one tooth, in the groin area.

"Olli, I said, trying to calm him down. "That's no way to make friends."

"Son-of-a-bitch," he said, leaving used to be one tooth and moving on to no tooth who was beginning to come around, starting to raise his head. Oliver's kick upside returned no tooth to la, la, land, which was an act of kindness thing for him. He never felt Olli's efforts to perform a kidney extraction via his beer belly using nothing but Reeboks as surgical instruments.

I made a mental note to get Oliver some help for his anger management issues. Now was probably not the time to bring it up.

"Come on Olliver," I said. We got to get the fuck out of here. These guys sister comes out here she'll kick the shit out of both of us."

"Son-of-a-bitch," Olli said, moving to the car still holding his rib cage with one arm. He wrestled his way into the car one armed with only about three more "son of a bitches," and slammed the door.

The old Chevy Impala made considerable haste to get us to the nearest area of town where we could safely stop and get some bandages for Oliver. He wasn't losing a lot of blood, but his head looked like it had spent some time in a sandblasting machine. Needed cleaned up.

"Jesus Christ," Oliver groaned.

"That's' good Olli. Your profanity vocabulary list is expanding. I was beginning to worry about brain damage. I thought they had kicked everything out of you but the statement "son-of-a-bitch."

I went through a red light. Several horns honked. In this neighborhood going through a red light was safer than stopping at one. Moving targets are harder to hit. "Maybe you should put your seat belt on Olly" I suggested. His look told me to go fuck myself. The thought did not require verbalization to be understood quite clearly.

He struggled to an upright position. Good indication he was coming around. "Why did you just leave me there with those god damn gorillas using me for a door mat?" Th expanding vocabulary of curse words now convinced me he was on the mend. "I think all of my damn ribs are broken." I gave him a minute as he struggled to get his breathing controlled and let him cool a bit.

"I do not believe ribs are not broken or you wouldn't be able scream profanities like that without puncturing a lung." I suggested. Olly groaned "piece of cake job, my arse".

"Oliver it is not my fault you get yourself balls deep into risky situations. What would you have me do Oliver? Jump right in there all macho and tough and get my ass kicked like yours. Hell no, Olli. I am not tough. I weigh one hundred and seventy pounds. About as much as one of those guys legs. If you are not tough like I am not tough, then you have to be smart."

My point needed emphasizing. "Look at this face Olli. You do not see many scars, do you? I stay this pretty by being smart."

"You had a gun. You could have just shot the fat bastards."

"You forget Oliver, I didn't have the gun; you had the gun. Besides, you cannot just go around shooting every fat bastard you have a disagreement with. Or skinny bastards either, for that matter. You shoot someone and the police get involved. Names get out. Their friends come and shoot you. Your friends go and shoot their friends. The whole thing snowballs and before you know it, everyone is shooting everyone else, and no one remembers why anyone is shooting anyone. It's much better to settle your differences over a nice bottle of wine. Or maybe two". I chuckled at my own joke trying to lighten the mood.

"Those fat bastards needed shot," he barked. "Shot and then pissed on."

"You really need to work on that anger issue you have Olli. Take some anger management classes."

"You take the classes. I'll shoot the fuckers", he growled.

"You can't shoot all the fuckers in this world Olli. There just is not enough bullets. Besides, you and I would be some of the first fuckers to go."

"And by the way, if you are so hell bent to shoot someone, where is the gun? Why didn't you shoot them? Could've saved me ten bucks on wine."

Olli was catching his breath and the adrenaline rush was giving way to the pain. He managed to get a shitty look on his face when I mentioned the gun.

"They got it," he finally said.

"They got it. How in the hell did they get it? Did they take it out of your hand when you were trying to shoot them?

"I gave it to them."

"You gave it to them. Why? Just so they could beat you up without worrying about getting shot."

"He asked nicely if he could look at it."

"Oh, that's good Olli. Next time someone is going to shoot us, we will just ask them nicely if we can look at their gun?

"Is that what the fight was over? He took your gun and wouldn't give it back."

"No, He asked for the gun, I gave him the gun, he whacked me on the side of the head with it. That is what the fight was over, and it wasn't really a fight. I never knew what hit me. The first fighting I done was when I sunk my teeth into that huge ham hock. I was just doing what you said. Using my infinite charm. It was working too. This one lady was being very open to me. In hindsight, I think maybe she belonged to one tooth."

"One tooth." I said, "He was too ugly to have a lady."

"This lady was none too easy to look at." He shook his head and shivered. "Ugh, the sacrifices I make for this job."

"Jesus Olli, not the waitress behind the bar." I didn't recall any other women in the bar.

"No, no, not her. He stopped. "Same dimensions. Better personality".

He thought about that for a second. "At least I thought so at the time."

"So, did you learn anything about Dustin Harcourt?"

"I learned that if you mention his name, people treated you like you had leprosy." He stopped.

"And then beat the shit out of you."

We stopped at a pharmacy and purchased some band aids and antiseptic for Oliver's wounds once we had reached a little safer neighborhood. Some swelling was becoming noticeable on Oliver's face, but he was never that pretty to look at before this adventure. The minor scrapes would heal and only serve to enhance his charismatic identity. Or so I told myself and Olly.

Having done some minor first aid in the parking lot on Olly's face, I dropped him off at his residence so he could clean his wounds properly and returned to my office / living accommodations. One shot of pirate piss and I was asleep.

CHAPTER

5

I was having a nice dream of Mexico when Olli started pounding on the office door at seven am. I contemplated ignoring him and going back to my dream, then contemplated shooting him but he had given our only gun to the Bobbsey twins. I let him in.

"Morning boss" he said.

"Piss off Olli," I said. "A deal is a deal". I had a hunch he had slept on it, contemplated the beating, and was here to renegotiate the twenty percent arrangement. Either that or he crapped in his bed, and I didn't care to discuss either.

Before he had time to reply, I said "You know what Olli, we don't have a gun. What would we do if those two friends you made yesterday showed up? What if the neighbor's cat wakes you up again? We need to be able to defend ourselves."

I found my pants, took two hundred bucks out of my wallet, and passed it to him. "While I make myself presentable, how about you go out and buy us a gun each?"

"Great idea Mister M. It's about time we achieved a little professionalism. What kind of private investigator doesn't carry a gun?"

"Ok," I replied. "Go buy us some professionalism to carry while I get dressed."

After Oliver left, I called Susan Harcourt and gave a very limited update on where we were spending her money. I left out the details concerning the limited respect Oliver was granted upon the mention of her presumed dead husbands name as well as the fact that it was very unlikely her husband had died in the vehicle and floated out a 3 inch gap between the roof and walls of his vehicle to float away at sea.

I believed there was a very good possibility her husband was dead, and it would be in both of our interests for his death to have been accidental. Insurance companies are very reluctant to pay out policies on people whose bodies have bullet holes in them, so a missing body is better than a body full of bullet holes. I trusted the Jackals to have the good sense to know that bullet holes were not conducive to successful insurance claims and to bash his head in then send him over a cliff in his car if they were trying to collect a debt in a roundabout fashion. So, if the Jackals, or anyone interested in collecting a debt were involved, why was there not a body in the vehicle with injuries possibly sustained in driving over a cliff in your car? Things were not adding up and the only good thing about that was it was keeping me employed.

Susan had not heard from her debt collectors yet, and Jessica Baird was unavailable until after lunch. For Susan's protection, and perhaps my own motives, I thought it best to put Oliver on her tail for a few days, or at least until the Jackals made contact. Oliver and Susan had yet to be introduced, and for a time, we would keep it that way.

Olli was like a kid at Christmas when he returned. "Look at this baby Boss", he made a show of pulling the biggest revolver I had ever seen from his coat. His grin changed from excitement to evil. Kind of frightening. "44-magnum, stop a grizzly bear in its tracks" he cooed.

"Jeez, that's great Olli, "I replied. "Now, if we are ever downtown and come across a grizzly bear, we don't have to worry."

He got a pouty look on his mug but said nothing.

"Jesus Christ Olli, you think you're dirty Harry or what. That thing must weigh six pounds. Imagine how it will feel when someone asks nicely to see it and then whacks you on the side of the head with it. Like getting hit with a baseball bat swung by Hank Aaron.

I could see I was pissing him off, which is not usually a good thing to do to someone holding a really big gun. Especially if that someone is the type of guy who shoots at the neighbor's cat in an apartment complex because it woke him up.

"Just jerking your chain Olli, relax, by the way you are healing well" I said. "And by the way, where is my gun. I hope you got me something I can conceal without carrying a duffle bag."

He stopped fondling the 44 caliber Howitzer and I knew it was bad news.

"Sorry Mister M, you didn't get one. This baby ate up all the money you gave me plus I had to chip in fifty bucks of my own."

Now he was pissing me off. I asked nicely if I could see the monstrosity so I could whack him on the side of the head with it. Give him credit. He wasn't about to fall for that again.

"Screw you," he said, "Nobody touches this baby but me."

I put on the best disgruntled employer look I could muster and said nothing. The silence got to him eventually.

"Relax big guy, here is what I was thinking," he relented.

Oliver thinking is not usually a good thing. It is what he does right before he does other things like shooting at the neighbor's cat or letting gorillas who despise you look at your gun.

"I'm thinking I'll just take this big gun, go back where I was yesterday, and ask if I could please have my boss's little gun back. When I show them this baby, they won't mess with me." The shitty, evil grin on his swollen and scraped face gave the appearance of pure evil with a good portion of insanity on the side.

Without being condescending, I tried to explain.

"Olliver, when someone shoots you dead with a little gun, you end up the same dead, as being dead when someone shoots you with a big gun. Who ends up dead usually has more to do with who shoots first, not who has a bigger gun.

And, how would I explain that you got shot dead with my little gun?",

He contemplated that thought for a moment.

"Ok, so I'll shoot him first."

"And what if he doesn't have my gun. Dead people can't tell you where it is."

"I'll wound him, ask him for your gun, then shoot him dead."

"You cannot wound people with that cannon. Shoot him in the foot and he will probably die." He shrugged, "hmm, occupational hazard for anyone who takes my gun I guess, because I am going to get your little gun back, boss." He stated with conviction, possibly fueled by embarrassment, or maybe just plain meanness.

It was time for me to do some thinking, so I looked up a picture of Susan Harcourt on the internet for Oliver, described her Mercedes car, gave him her address. I gave him the Impala keys, and a bit of instruction on following her, undetected. He left assuring me the Impala and Susan would be diligently cared for by him and his big gun. No harm would come to either.

I would have to drive one of McCurdy Inc.'s back up vehicles. Said vehicles being a choice of a ten-speed bicycle, or a well used and often crashed, Honda 350 cc street bike.

With Oliver's departure, I settled in to do some thinking.

I searched for the eraser for the white board on my wall, then rubbed the grocery list and other important data off with my shirt sleeve, and then, contemplated the facts of the case so far.

What I wrote was:

Dustin Harcourt

- Missing- dead or otherwise??? Not dead from car accident.
- Rich. Unknown association with Jackals. What is association??
- Jackals- 2-million-dollar debt. What for??
- Marries small Midwest farm girl- motive?? What is up with that?
- Ten-million-dollar life insurance policy on self?? Why?

Susan Harcourt

- Marries playboy with shady background. For the love?? Maybe, maybe not.
- Very bright- innocent or maybe not??

Jessica Baird

- Who the hell was she, and why give a glowing reference for McCurdy Investigations Inc.? Financially they could afford the biggest agency in town with far more resources, even if I hesitated to admit they may be better qualified. Why me??? Is it possible they wanted to buy some integrity on top of the confidentiality agreement that all investigators were bound by?

The Jackals

- What was their involvement? Did Oliver's newfound acquaintances have Jackals connections, or was it just Oliver's natural charms that pissed them off?

All this thinking was stressing me out. A little relaxation seemed to be in order, so I opened a mickey of rum. About half-way through the mickey, I had a startling revelation. If my instincts served me correct, and, after half mickey of rum they were usually spot-on, Susan Harcourt may be in danger. Good thing I had posted Oliver on watch.

CHAPTER 6

The half mickey of rum relaxed me to a state where my body desired a short power nap, disregarding my brains desire to get some meaningful work done.

My cell phone vibrated and barked like a dog. I had changed the ringer from a duck as Oliver thought a dog barking sounded more private eye professional. I awoke with a start, dreaming of the junkyard dogs who wished to have me for lunch. I noted that 2 hours had passed.

I answered the phone/ It was Olly.

"Boss, that pretty lady is out of her house, in her Mercedes, and on the move"

"Good job Olly, stick with her and see where she goes."

"I know that Mister M, Jeez, shut up and listen". He paused. "Reason I called is, I don't think I am the only one following her. There was a big Cadillac been sitting by her house. When she left, it pulled out and followed her. Now I am following behind the Cadillac that is following behind her. Cadillac windows are all dark and I can't see who is inside".

I was instantly alert. "Scary shit Oliver, keep her safe, and stay in touch, I am on my way. Where are you now and where are you headed?"

"We are all heading north on industrial drive. Looks like we may be heading towards that nice part of town we were at yesterday. And, no worries, me and grizzly stopper won't let any harm come to Ms. Harcourt."

Contrary to that statement, my worry meter climbed into the red danger zone. Oliver's conflict resolution talents, most often, involved some form of violence. A good outcome would be if the object of his conflict was rendered unconscious. I had the feeling he was itching to test his grizzly bear stopper. Not good. I would have to check into the availability of anger management, and conflict resolution classes for him.

The Honda was stored in my garage, AKA garden shed, along with some shovels, rakes, lawn mower, and other necessary tools of the private investigator trade, in the rear of the building. I went down the stairs 3 at a time, removed the padlock, and mounted the bike. It fired up first kick as always. The helmet was hanging on the handlebars so for lack of a better place to put it, I set it on my head. I had neglected to send the bike for repairs after the last crash it was involved in, and the right signal light was dangling by the wires from where it used to be attached. The left signal light was missing, along with the windshield and various other decorative pieces. What the bike lacked in good looks, it made up for in agility and maneuverability on the city streets, back alleys, or the pedestrian and bike lanes, as the urgency of the arrival time necessitated. The urgency in this case was dictated by the protection of my client along with any number of innocent bystanders, in addition to possibly some preventative measures to keep Olly from shooting up the streets with his new cannon.

Utilizing a couple of back alleys, ignoring stop signs and red lights, and only needing to enter the pedestrian lanes/sidewalks temporarily on a couple of occasions, I was able to intercept the little convoys route of travel within 15 minutes. I watched as first Susan Harcourts car passed, followed by the Cadillac, followed by Oliver in the Impala.

I kept my distance, following as discreetly as was possible, given my mode of transportation but should have known I could not evade Olly's keen eye. Several blocks into my tailing, my cell phone vibrated and barked in my shirt pocket. I freed up my left hand from driving to accept the call and put it on speaker phone.

It was Olly. "Boss, now we seem to have some idiot on a street bike joined our little group of travellers. He is trying to be inconspicuous and pretend he is not following behind me but is obviously not very adept at the art of surveillance."

"Oliver, that idiot is me" I shouted over the noise of the bike. Part of the muffler was missing as well.

"Oh" Olly replied, "Sorry about that boss, didn't recognize you with your helmet on"

"Whatever Olly, stick with the program" I shouted. I was not about to let the comment about my surveillance talents pass however now did not seem to be the time for a battle of wits.

"Okay boss, you be careful on that bike. The thing is dangerous. Last time I rode it I crashed it". The dangling signal light tapped my knee as a reminder.

Olly ended the call just as Susan slowed to turn into the parking lot of a what appeared to be an abandoned warehouse. Two stories high, no windows on the upper floor, ground floor windows boarded over, and one entrance door not covered, with a faded to illegible sign above it which had probably said administration or office once upon a time. I idled to the curb and parked. I could make a more-stealthy approach on foot than on a bike with a broken muffler.

Oliver had passed by the first approach into the parking lot which Susan had entered and parked illegally in front of the other entrance effectively using the Impala to block off the approach and the Cadillacs likely exit point. Susan, unwisely, parked in front of the doorway and the Cadillac angled behind her blocking her retreat. I would have to have a discussion with her on being prepared for evasive tactics when dealing these folks.

There was a short but thick hedge on my side of the lot. I crouched down, and moved with much stealth on my knees behind the hedge to a position about 50 feet from the vehicles, lay on my belly and peaked through the hedge so I could observe without being seen. I wished I had my gun. What transpired was rather anti-climactic for the moment. The passenger door of the Cadillac opened, and

I recognized the recent acquaintance who exited. Judging by the swollen lips and unhealed scaring around the lips and chin, I assumed it was the recipient of my wine bottle dental procedure. I also assumed the driver was likely to be the original "No tooth", the second of the Bobbsey twins Oliver had been making friends with. Scar lips approached Susan's door, she rolled the window down, and was handed a package. The only words spoken were by my recent acquaintance. "Keep it with you at all times, answer it when it rings. Keep it charged. Charger is in the box". He retreated to the car door he had left open, squeeze his bulk inside, and the Cadillac moved ahead allowing Susan to back out and exit the lot via the same approach she had entered. All good. I assumed it was a burner phone which would be the Jackals method of contacting her for delivery of payment. At least Susan was out of harms way for the time being.

The Cadillac was moving but made no effort to follow Susan in the Mercedes. I was using my stealth talents crawling back to the Honda when things went south. I heard Oliver shout "stop", then the roar of his miniature cannon. I looked over the hedge in time to see the Cadillac, steam rising from the bullet hole in radiator, accelerate towards Olly, who was standing in the path of the caddy holding the gun in a two-handed stance pointing at the oncoming vehicle.

The Bobbsey twins were no strangers to evasive maneuvers themselves and gravel flew from the cars back tires as it sped towards Oliver. Olly done a barrel roll to his right, that would be the envy of any stuntman, avoiding the speeding Cadillac. The driver of the Cadillac who I assumed to be "No tooth" made a valiant effort to swerve around the Impala Oliver had thoughtfully stationed in the exit to block traffic, to no avail. The older model Cadillac outweighed the Impala by about a ton, and its momentum pushed the Impala sideways to the far curb. The Impala provided enough interference to deflect the Caddy's forward advance into the metal light pole firmly anchored at the approaches entrance. Oliver was up in an instant and in hot pursuit. The doors on the Cadillac flew open and both no tooth and newly named Scar lips showed amazing agility and speed as they ran from the vehicle inspired no doubt by the roar of Olly's cannon. In seconds they had passed through a hedge and out of Oliver's line of site. Oliver kept moving until he reached the Cadillac, then realizing he could never catch up to them fired a couple random shots, near as I could figure, just to hear the sound.

He stopped and looked in the Caddy. He ruffled around in the car for a moment, then came back out, turning towards me with a huge, shitty, grin on his face.

"Hey boss, look what I found" He held up the gun he had given to the Bobbsey twins yesterday between two fingers.

"That's great Olly, just fucking great" I said. I realized I was speaking louder than necessary and in fact, it was probably as loud as I was able. "Now we have two guns and no fucking car. Just look at the Impala. Three fucking hours you've had it and it is totally fucked" I said as I approached. I tried to slam the door that was hanging open to emphasize my point to no avail. It creaked and sprung back on the first attempt, second attempt it fell off.

Olly's elation at finding the gun faded from his face along with the shitty grin as it dawned on him, he had just sacrificed a 5000-dollar car and our only means of transportation excepting a small street bike and a 10 speed bicycle for a 100 dollar gun.

"So, just tell me Oliver, what do we do now? We are to meet with Ms. Harcourt and Jessica Baird, her lawyer, in less than an hour. How do you propose we do that? Not to mention neglecting our client who may be in danger with no support from us. Jesus H Christ, what were you thinking? And besides all that I am pretty sure you have hurt those guys feelings again, and they will not want to be friends anymore."

"Jeez boss, settle down, you are going to have a stroke. It is just a car". What I really wanted was to do was take a stroke at Olly but he outweighed me by at least 90 lbs.

He approached me cautiously and held out the gun as a peace offering. "Look boss, even has bullets in it. More than I had in it. Loaded up, right full". I took the gun from his hand and contemplated shooting him in the toe or some other place that would be a non-fatal wound with my little 38 caliber gun. I could only push Oliver's guilt trip so far before his temper would overrule any emotional considerations and the very real possibility of him returning fire with his big gun not intending to wound deterred those thoughts.

Olly's face contorted into a strained look as though he was struggling to take a big crap indicating his problem-solving skills were being heavily taxed when he said "Insurance boss, you must have insurance. It is totalled for sure this time. They will never be able to tell it had been sideswiped on both sides before." He always smiled when planning something sneaky, evil, or conniving.

"Yeah Olly, I have insurance, but insurance doesn't get us to our meeting on time. And the vehicle was illegally parked in a travel way by someone which may cause them to question why and who the legal driver was which brings up the question, do you have a drivers licence Oliver?"

"Yes Boss, I can legally drive anything on wheels. Even got my licence to drive semi trucks at one time when I was thinking it might be easier to earn a living that way than being a private investigator. People do not usually shoot at truck drivers".

"Serious", I said, I had just learned a little something. Add a few minutes to my life expectancy.

It is hard to stay mad at Oliver when he is acting like a scolded puppy even if I knew it was just an act. After few minutes and a little more profanity, the urgency of our situation dawned on me. "It is what it is Olly, and we have to make the best of it. Get on the bike behind me".

The Honda was riding very low with my 170 lbs in the front, and Oliver's 250 lbs on the back. Especially on the back. I had to lean forward on the handlebars to reduce the possibility of it flipping over backwards. Olly didn't have the lean and balance quite figured out, so maneuverability suffered a bit, but we were moving in the right direction all be it, a bit slowly.

CHAPTER 7

Dustin Harcourt Holdings office building, where we were to meet with Ms. Harcourt and her lawyer Jessica Baird, was in a substantially more affable part of the city. Despite our not quite legal, overloaded mode of transportation, Oliver and I arrived unmolested by law, or other thugs without the badges. I parked the Honda in the rear of the building hoping no one was watching our arrival. As Oliver noted, we did not look like professional FBI type investigators so much as we looked like a poverty stricken, larger and heavier version, of Cheech and Chong. I noted that neither of us had a beard more than one day growth, and personally, my clothing was all intact. Oliver had left part of his shirt and a bit of skin in the gravel while executing his barrel roll out of the way of the Caddy. His complexion was somewhat marred from the encounter yesterday with

No tooth and Scar lips but I consoled him with the fact that I thought it was healing rather nicely and not likely to leave any permanent scarring. What do I know, I am not a dermatologist or a doctor and besides that, his penchant for attracting trouble made it unlikely his future endeavors would put his face on the cover of Gentlemen's quarterly magazine. Work on your personality Oliver, it will be with you a lot longer than your good looks anyway I suggested. I am not sure he took that advice to heart.

Security met us upon entering the double glass doors which was good to see, even though it took some convincing of the security guard that we actually had an appointment. After a short wait while he made a phone call upstairs to confirm we were the dynamic duo expected for the 1:00 o'clock appointment and he reluctantly let us pass unescorted to the elevator, cautioning us not to stop on any floors other than the top one where Jessica Baird's office was located. We had no intention of making any pit stops I assured him; however, it still made me wonder why the advice was necessary. Olly may have looked a bit frightening but not to the stage people would leap out windows if he appeared at their door.

The bell chimed indicating we had arrived at our destination floor, and the elevator doors opened to a luxuriously decorated suite with a smiling receptionist to greet us. The smile may have been from years of practice and not completely genuine but never wavered as she said, "Mr. McCurdy and Mr. Barnett I assume." I nodded in the affirmative.

"Susan and Jessica are expecting you. I will notify them you have arrived." She turned her attention to the desk phone and spoke quietly, "A Mr. McCurdy and Mr. Barnett to see you."

She turned back to us with the permanent smile. "Please take a seat, someone will be with you shortly".

Susan arrived to escort us to the meeting room. She done a double take at Oliver's embattled appearance and at the grizzly stopper he tried to hide by tucking into his belt and letting his shirt hang over it, but she concealed any disdain she may have had rather well.

I formally introduced Oliver as my partner, and they shook hands with the usual formalities, excepting the fact, that Oliver's jaw was hanging open in awe and I worried his tongue may fall out onto his chin when Susan said, "Mr. Barnett, delighted to make your acquaintance". Lacking the use of his tongue, Oliver mumbled something I am sure was meant to mean "Likewise."

Susan seated us in a board room meant to hold many more people than would be attending today. I am not a connoisseur of art forms, but the room was adorned with several items not included in most business settings. There were vases that to my untrained eye may or may not have been from the Ming dynasty but definitely were of Chinese origin, or at least design. One wall was adorned with a rug that my interpretation would have been Persian. Looked like a damn magic carpet. Whatever it was, I doubted it came from Walmart. There were also paintings that looked like originals and probably done by famous artists if I had known the name of any famous artists. Susan offered to let us seat anywhere we wished so we moved around the table to have our backs to the wall, more from force of habit than any indication we may require it.

Jessica Baird arrived momentarily, and Susan made the introductions. Jessica Baird was tall, slim dark haired, large brown eyes and a guess at her age would have been early thirty something-ish. Very stylishly and expensively dressed. My brain confirmed that I would not have forgotten meeting her before and with the glowing reference still fresh in my mind, I stood, and said " Jessica, good to see you again": offering my hand.

She hesitated momentarily, quickly regained her composure, and changed the subject, but it was enough to confirm the glowing reference she provided came from a google search of not so reputable investigators, not from any dealings we may have had in the past.

She quickly took control of the meeting.

"As I am sure everyone here understands we may be discussing some rather sensitive information here today that must not be disclosed outside these walls so I have taken the liberty of drawing up this confidentiality agreement for everyone. Please read and sign." She stated, passing around the forms.

Discretion goes without saying in the investigations business however, the lady was a corporate lawyer and may have been just acting out of habit. I did not want to read to much into it so took the form, pretended I was a speed reader, signed it and passed it back without having read more than a couple lines of the legal blather lawyers use to make you think they put a lot of effort into something so they can charge an exorbitant fee. Sort of like a pinky swear with consequences. Oliver did likewise. I noted that Olly and I did not receive copies. Regardless, I was sure Jessica had at least 10 million good reasons, and possibly more, to keep today's discussion confidential.

Jessica addressed Susan. "Susan, I realize this may be difficult for you considering the recent loss of your husband so if you wish to leave the room at anytime, please do so. Your involvement is absolutely necessary as the designated corporate head of the company as well as the prime contact with the extortionists whoever they may be, however, if you feel the need for a break at anytime, we will oblige."

I observed that Susan was maintaining her composure rather well for a recent widow. Tough cookie.

Jessica continued. "The facts are That Dustin Harcourt is missing and presumed deceased, a very large insurance policy is at stake and currently being reviewed by the Insurance company, which like all insurance companies do not like to pay out policies without a detailed investigation and absolute proof of the circumstances. Mr. McCurdy and Mr. Barnett, we have entrusted you with the task of providing that proof. I have discussed with Susan, and we are prepared to offer you a ten percent commission of the insurance claim for successfully providing confirmation of death and proof that the circumstances were accidental. Even though we are confident the nature of Dustin's death was accidental, with no body to confirm it, we rely on your professionalism for that confirmation.

In addition to that, we have a group of unknown persons attempting to extort a rather large sum and if it is necessary to pay that out of the insurance claim, we would require that you receive your percentage of what remains of the insurance value after deducting the portion paid out to the extortionists.

The coincidence of the extortion attempt and the death of Mr. Harcourt may serve to arouse suspicion with the insurance group and for that reason we have determined that police involvement would be unwise."

No shit, I thought but held my tongue. Oliver's mouth was clamped shut due to the shortage of skin on his face. His eyes were stretched open so wide as he calculated the ten percent commission offer that they were using all of the skin available. I knew there was going to be disagreement over his twenty percent portion of the payout but there was enough money to leave some room for negotiations between us at a later time.

Jessica continued. "So, Gentlemen, you are tasked with two very important missions that will be mutually beneficial to both parties. Number one priority task is to provide conclusive proof of the accidental demise of our dear Mr. Harcourt, and number two task, is to avoid payment to the extortionists. Are you in agreement to the terms and are you confident you can fulfill the obligations outlined?"

"Yes", Oliver blurted before I had a chance to speak.

"Ms. Baird," I interjected as Oliver scowled at me. "I agree with my esteemed colleague that McCurdy Investigations is up to the tasks described, however there are some extenuating circumstances that make this a high-risk operation. Our experiences over the last couple days indicate that we are dealing with some rather unscrupulous individuals or groups who have little respect for the law or common human decency for that matter. Please note the evidence of this on Mr. Barnett's face, body, and clothing, as he has been required to defend himself on numerous occasions as of late. Just this morning, unbeknownst to Susan, we were following her to ensure her safety which resulted in an altercation in which our vehicle was destroyed and Oliver, through his own agility and skill was able to avoid even more grievous harm than his injuries attest to. To keep the investigation moving forward uninterrupted there may be some incidental costs such as vehicle rentals and possibly medical bills we would require in the event of the remote possibility the insurance is not paid in which case our commission would be nil. We would request these costs be covered on an as required basis.

"Of course, Jessica replied, we have complimentary vehicles available for our out-of-town clients. See the receptionist when you leave here, and I will have her arrange the use of these as you require. She will require a valid driver's licence and ID. We would hope there would be no medical expenses, but should they occur, we will relent and ensure these are covered as well, however it will only cover costs for yourselves and not any other individuals that may be injured."

I thought of adding funeral expenses as well but after consideration thought that may be a bit much and may bring our confidence level into question. And may also worry Oliver if that was possible to do so.

I paused as though I may be having second thoughts knowing full well my own greed and shortage of common sense had over-ruled any objections, I may have had some time ago.

"Ok, it is agreed then. Now moving forward, to update the situation, our investigation thus far indicates the "unknown extortionists you reference" are in all probability, most likely in fact, the well-known Jackals group judging by the stationary they provided the initial communication on. I doubt anyone would be unwise enough to impersonate them, and Mr. Barnett's investigations into this group, are what lead to some confrontation resulting in his injuries and as well, his feelings have been hurt as he is a non-violent and articulate individual with the excellent communication skills, diplomacy, and the highest level of integrity." A blatant lie but not uncommon within my chosen profession. Oliver managed to turn his neck far enough to stare at the side of my head as though I was from another planet.

"As mentioned, I continued, we had followed Susan this morning and are aware of the burner phone with which she has been provided. For this reason, I would suggest that Susan be provided with twenty-four-hour security and I would designate my colleague Oliver to provide that service. Perhaps he could provide chauffer services to her as a pretense."

That turned Olly's scowl upside down.

Jessica hesitated glancing at Susan, Susan spoke for the first time. "I have no issue with that and with everything that has happened, I would feel more secure. I know you should not judge people by their looks but the people I met this morning did not present a comforting image. What came to mind when I saw them was rabid dogs excepting neither had any teeth."

"Ok that is agreed then which leads to my next question.

"Do you have access to the 2 million dollars in cash demanded by the extortionists, or is that dependent on the insurance money? They have asked that it be ready in two days and the insurance will not be paid out in that time frame."

Susan looked towards Jessica. "It can be arranged" Jessica finally stated after much fidgeting. She did not appear to be happy about it but did not elaborate.

"Ok then, I would suggest you start to arrange that Jessica."

And finally, "Would it be possible for me to have a copy of the last will and testament, and possibly the insurance documents?"

Jessica interjected before Susan could speak.

"A last will and testament is a confidential and deeply personal document. I do not believe it would be appropriate to share. Suffice to say that Susan is the sole heir. As a corporate entity our insurance documents are vast, however I will try to arrange for you to view the insurance document pertaining to Dustin's death."

I have been accused of having a deeply suspicious nature and always considered it complimentary seeing as the business I was in. I have also had some dealings with legal jargon contained in wills, namely my mothers, in which there were conditions attached. For me to be the recipient of the lawn mower and garden shed my mother bequeathed to me, it was necessary for me to out survive her by 15 days otherwise shed and lawnmower would revert to the executors of the estate. I know it was not a condition my mother put in there and when I asked the lawyer what the hell was up with that, he simply stated it was a common practice. Not a big deal considering the value of a lawnmower and shed was relatively low compared to a ten-million-dollar life insurance policy in addition to however many more millions in real estate value.

"Ok then, can you tell me if there are any conditions attached to Susan's inheritance?

Jessica skillfully dodged the question. "It is a standard last will and testament format."

My forementioned suspicious nature suggested it may be best to have Jessica believe I had accepted her explanation when quite the opposite had happened. My spider senses were tingling. More of "something is wrong with this picture" floating around the back of my brain.

I addressed Susan.

"Ok then, if no one has anything to add, we will get back to work on this case."

Jessica, smiled. "If I may make a suggestion, perhaps Mr. Barnett's first duty as Susan's chauffer may be to chauffer Susan to someplace where she could assist Mr. Barnett in choosing some more appropriate chauffer attire."

Oliver looked down and studied his clothing. "I'm ok with that" he said.

Susan stood, "I will accompany you out and we can stop and get you keys for a vehicle on the way."

"Much obliged mam", I said motioning for her to lead, ladies first as the saying goes. Oliver pushed in front of me to follow Susan. I was unsure whether his motivation was dedication to duty, or just for the better view.

CHAPTER

8

I had a choice between Mercedes and BMW offered. I would have preferred a pickup but did nor press the point. The places I was likely to travel in the near future was more suited to "good ole boy" transportation. Driving a BMW or Mercedes was apt to raise suspicion among my peers or the tax collectors who constantly hounded me, not to mention they were more likely to be stolen or at least vandalized, and the driver mugged.

Oliver, Susan, and I, had parted company in the parking lot, Oliver grinning like a kid on Xmas morning behind the wheel of the Mercedes heading out to shop for Chauffer clothes.

I took the opportunity of doing a lap past the location of this morning's encounter while test driving my new wheels. There were tow trucks attached to both vehicles, lights flashing and police attending the scene. I recognized the officer in charge as Sargent Morgan and contemplated a quick retreat. I had failed to endear myself to Sargent Morgan on previous encounters.

He approached my vehicle, "Well, well, if it isn't Mr. Shits and giggles McCurdy. I was about to put out an all points bulletin on you seeing as you were not at the scene of an accident in which a vehicle registered to your company was involved. Let me think what charges may be forthcoming in your future. How about we start with leaving the scene of an accident".

I interrupted. "I am sorry officer Morgan, but as you can see, I have other transportation and was unaware that this vehicle registered in my company name was not sitting in front of my office where it was parked when I left it this morning. If that is indeed my vehicle, it is hard to tell it is so badly damaged, then it must have been stolen sometime after I left. "Well, isn't that a coincidence McCurdy. The licence plates are registered in your name. Two vehicles involved in a collision, and both stolen and not a soul around. A Cadillac that had plates that belonged to a Toyota which was actually reported stolen two days ago, and your vehicle which you are just reporting as stolen now. Radiator of Cadillac has a bullet hole in it. Don't see any holes in your beater but hard to tell its such a piece of junk." He paused to spit. "You are full of shit McCurdy and you, and I both know it. I offered no comment. "So…, now that we have that clearly established, I hear you have been sticking your nose in on another vehicle accident I attended recently. A nearly new Mercedes. Shame to wreck a nice car like that."

That was the first time Officer Morgan and I had ever agreed on anything. I stated as much and mentioned how great minds think alike.

"I consider that an insult McCurdy. Your mind floats around in pirate piss and mine is invigorated by 12-year-old scotch. So, shove it up your ass. Seeing as I have you here, and just out of mutual disrespect, I would caution you to keep your nose out of other people's business." He lowered his voice. "The Dustin Harcourt business more specifically. I would not want you to come to any harm that would prevent me from locking up your sorry ass someday"

"So nice we could have this chat and I sincerely appreciate your concern for my welfare officer Morgan" I smiled.

He patted the sill below the rolled down window of the car. "It's Sargent Morgan, now Fuck off McCurdy" he advised.

I took his advice.

Confident that Oliver would ensure the safety of Susan wherever they may travel, I returned to the office to do a bit of research on Dustin Harcourt. I found a recent picture of him at the opening of a new building event. Although not in the same handsome league I considered myself to be in, I supposed he could be considered tall dark, and handsome by a Midwest farm girl. I could find very little history on him, or how he had climbed to the top in the real estate business. No educational background to indicate he was a Harvard graduate or even a community college graduate. Not that you needed education to get rich, you could be born rich, or lucky rich, marry rich, or just in the right place at the right time rich. I failed on all counts, and could find no indication what category Dustin Harcourt fell in. Of course, you could also steal rich, but you needed to be smart and lucky to stay rich if that was your preferred method. Susan was about to become very rich and was dependent on me and Oliver to be smart if she were going to be rich. To be on the safe side my first concern would be to make sure she was stay alive rich. In order of priorities, Susan's safety topped the list, followed by getting the Jackals out of the picture, followed by some innovative thinking and imaginative documentation to prove Dustin Harcourt had succumbed to a tragic accident of some sort. To ensure the success of priority number one would necessitate that no one be trusted at this stage. I would have to utilize my newly acquired expense account and invest in some electronics toys. My gut was telling me there was much more to the story than Susan knew or was able to divulge to McCurdy Investigations. I google searched until I found a supplier for the items I would need. Interesting name. Fly on the wall security supplies. It was located in a commercial district with large shopping malls and would be the perfect place for me to have an enjoyable shopping experienced, just as the mall advertised. I called Oliver to touch base and let him know a bit about my intentions.

Traffic was relatively light, and I was at my destination for an enjoyable shopping experience within the half hour. I chose a relatively central location of the mall parking lot to park the pickup truck. One reason was that mall parking lots seem to be designed for compact cars and not full size vehicles. I made my way across the lot to the double glass door entrance. Upon entering I was immediately surrounded by hordes of people having and enjoyable shopping experience. I stopped in a store that advertised sporting goods and purchased a Dodgers baseball cap and oversize sunglasses. I put both on, made my way across the mall as quickly as I could and exited through the double glass doors on the opposite side. From there it was a ten-minute walk to my personal enjoyable shopping experience destination. Fly on the wall security supplies. The shop owner and I had met before. "What are you here to cheap out on today, McCurdy?" he asked. "No cheap out today buddy, I want nothing but top of the line." I gave him my supply list.

"Ah, impressive he observed", as he left to gather the requested items. He returned and rang up all the items which amounted to an exorbitant amount. I could not help but comment. "You are sure you haven't got one too many zeros on there buddy/? Seems pricey for that little bit of stuff." He just smiled. "Nothing but the best for Shits and giggles investigators" Jesus Christ, did everybody know the smart-ass blabbermouth ex of mine.

I could not argue that I deserved the best and seeing as it was on the expense account, I paid, placed the items in the sporting goods store bag I brought with me and left for the short walk back to the mall. I stepped through the doors into the mob of customers, removed the hat and glasses, put them in the bag, and exited the opposite doors back to the pickup. One half hour total shopping. Mall advertisement was right. It was an enjoyable experience.

Next stop was a wand car wash. I waited my turn and entered. The attendant closed the door behind me. The car did not really need washed but I gave it a quick rinse for appearances if someone was watching, then put some batteries in the toy I had purchased. Guaranteed to locate any and all tracking devices. The equipment done as advertised. The tracker was magnetic and attached to the frame behind the front bumper. I was reasonably sure we would find the same when we scanned Susan's Mercedes.

I left the tracker attached where it was. Having the opponent think they knew where you were at all times can be an advantage as long as you know that they think they know. They would know where the vehicle was and therefore assume the occupant was nearby. Having them think they knew where Susan was at all times would allow us to relocate her, thus giving us an upper hand towards keeping her safe. Priority one. We would not be able to do that until after Susan received further instructions from the extortionists. I needed to get her and Oliver to meet me somewhere away from prying eyes and ears that so that we could have a confidential conversation involving the only three people I trusted. Oliver, Susan, and myself.

Meanwhile I would do my best to encourage the illusion of incompetence which I was beginning to suspect may have been the reason we were hired rather than my stellar record. The trackers could have been planted at anytime after we left Harcourt holdings building, or…. was it before we left? I was having trouble sorting the good guys from the bad guys so until confirmed otherwise, everyone would have to be considered the bad guys. The Jackals, Harcourt holdings, and what was up with the caution from Sargent Morgan? What in hell could he possibly know that would inspire him to give ne a warning. Or was it a threat? I doubted he was really concerned for my well being seeing as we had a long history of disrespect for each other.

I needed to talk to my esteemed colleague Oliver. It was time for me to take a walk in the park, get a little exercise to maintain my superb physical condition. Whoever was tracking our movements may also be monitoring our conversations. The electronics industry made some great toys for those engaged in subterfuge, fraud, deceit, and trickery when you were the one using them. Someone else directing there use towards your own privacy, maybe not so great.

Oliver tended to take words quite literally and people who made derogatory or offensive comments to him in jest, were often reminded to be more cordial when addressing him about the time one of his ham fists met their face. It would take some diplomatically worded cunning and conniving on my part to lure him to a safe zone for speaking without him altering my shockingly handsome face. I headed back to my office. I find I am more proficient at cunning and conniving after a couple shots of rum.

A couple shots of rum later and I had a plan. Not necessarily a great plan, but a plan none the less. I would have a discussion with him, but no words were to be spoken except words that we were ok with others listening to. I called Oliver's cell phone. He picked up on the first ring.

"Oliver Barnett speaking" he answered cordially. Christ, what had she done to him? His normal greeting was more likely to be a loud WHAT! Or WTF you want now?

"Hi Oliver, I trust everything is going well with you and that Susan has no issues you people have had no trouble or delivery instructions as of yet."

"Everything is great boss. No issues of any kind. Susan is great and no contact with extortionist vermin bastards yet. I am great. Living the dream. Drive fancy cars, dress all nice, and all I have to do is protect a beautiful girl. Easy if you got the professionalism we purchased right here in a holster under my jacket. No one dare threaten to harm this lady while I am on duty. I'm thinking this may be a new career direction for me." He sounded almost giddy. He provided a great set up for my diplomatic conniving. "Yes Oliver, and I have been thinking, now that we are getting more professional and moving into the big leagues and you have proven time and again what a great asset you are to McCurdy investigations, it may be time to renegotiate that 20% arrangement." There was silence on the line for a few seconds. Finally, he spoke. "You ok boss? Where are you? How drunk are you?"

"I'm fine Oliver, and I am at the office, and, uhm, not very drunk. We need to discuss this in person. When can you make it into the office?"

"Boss, I am on duty here, I cannot leave Susan unprotected."

"Of course not, Oliver, and I wouldn't expect a professional such as yourself to neglect your duties. I was thinking maybe Susan could come with you, sit in on our negotiations as an independent observer while she waits for the bad guys to call. She is just as safe here as she is at home as long as you are around, and it might take her mind off her troubles for awhile."

"I will check with the Boss, I mean Ms. Harcourt to see what her availability is like." He covered the phone but not well enough I could not hear him. "Boss Harcourt Mam, McCurdy investigation requests our presence at their office, at your convenience of course."

I could hear her reply. "Of course, Olly, whenever is convenient for you, be good to get away from all this waiting on a call for a while. It is making me stir crazy. I can bring the phone with me. It is fully charged."

Oliver shouted back. "We are about a half hour drive from there so how does 4 o'clock sound? "Works for me" she shouted back.

Oliver came back on the line. "Ms. Harcourt will be able to attend your appointment a 4pm Mr. McCurdy.

"Great, we shall see you both then." I hung up before my check valve screwed up and I said something sarcastic.

At precisely 4pm there was a knock on my door. Olly never knocked on my door before, just barged in like he owned the place and started blathering whatever was on his mind. Susan was creating a monster.

The change in his habit confused me and I was not sure what to do. Finally, I yelled "come in". Seemed to work.

The door opened and Susan entered followed by Oliver gawking around like he expected to find someone hiding in the junk strewn office, clearing the zone so to speak.

"Please have a seat", I motioned to the two chairs I had positioned directly in front of my desk.

Oliver seated Susan, then after checking my bathroom for anyone who may be lurking there, took up a position beside her.

Oliver was dressed in formal chauffer attire was my best guess. Except for the big bulge by the breast pocket where his holster stored the grizzly stopper, he looked like he had mugged a fucking organ grinders monkey and stole its clothing. I reminded myself that Olly was not good at accepting criticism, kept a straight face and said, "Nice suit".

"You like it. I picked it out myself."

"I thought you might have, now it is time to get down to business. Susan we appreciate you coming here as a witness to these negotiations."

It was time to initiate phase two of my devious and cunning plan. "If you will give me a moment, I will explain my thoughts on your qualifications Oliver.

I held up the first sheet of paper I had prepared.

In Printed block letters it said.

WE ARE BEING TRACKED AND POSSIBLY OUR CONVERSATION MONITORED. DO NOT SPEAK JUST YET. They both fidgeted but did not speak.

Second sheet.

WE WILL PRETEND TO NEGOTIATE A NEW PERCENTAGE AGREEMENT FOR OLIVER WHILE WE HAVE OUR DICSUSSION IN WRITING

I handed each a pen.

"So Oliver, We have worked together for some time now and agree that your skill set is ideally suited to your position with McCurdy"

Third sheet. I passed to Susan

HAVE YOU HAD A CHANCE TO CHECK FOR CONDITIONS ON THE LAST WILL AND TESTAMENT.

"What kind of increase would you think is fair Oliver?"

Oliver replied while Susan wrote.

I was thinking 50-50 would be fair seeing as I work as many hours as you.

Susan passed the sheet back to me. She had printed.

Only condition is that I out-survive Dustin by 15 days. WTF? If I do not survive the required 15 days it goes to the executors of the estate.

"Well Oliver, as I said, your services are invaluable but obviously there is overhead such as the office, vehicles and such that must be covered. I was thinking more like 25%.

Fourth sheet

I WAS THINKING MAYBE WE COULD MEET ON THE BEACH WHERE WE COULD HAVE A CONFIDENTIAL TALK WHERE WE WERE SURE WE ARE ALONE AND NO PLACE FOR ANY LISTENING DEVICES TO HIDE. DO YOU LIKE THE BEACH SUSAN?

I passed the sheet to Susan.

While Oliver said "Well I guess you have a point, How about 35%? Susan wrote.

I go to Bender's beach all the time.

While I said "Maybe 25% might be doable" Oliver took the sheet from Susan and wrote

You Cannot swim Boss.

I scribbled **"Fuck off Olly"** and passed it back with a grin to match his shitty grin. He was catching on. He said "I will have to think on it for a day. Is that ok?"

"Sure of course I said: as I passed sheet four.

Sheet four

OLIVER I AM GOING TO GIVE YOU MY SCANNER TO CHECK FOR BUGS AND TRACKING DEVICES ON THE MERCEDES AND IN SUSANS HOME. DO NOT REMOVE ANY THAT YOU FIND. BE VERY CAREFUL WHAT YOU SAY WHEN YOU LEAVE HERE UNTIL THAT IS DONE.

THERE IS A LOUNGE AT BENDERS BEACH. CAN WE MEET THERE AT 7PM? IT IS OK TO TALK ABOUT THAT

"Ok then, while you consider the offer Oliver, I will pass this on to my accountant and see if he thinks it is feasible" I said.

Susan wrote yes on the sheet and passed it to Oliver.

"I spoke. On another note, Susan I am assuming you have had no call from the extortionists as of yet, and it is reaching their original time limit so expect to hear something very soon. Has Jessica rounded up the cash for the payment when they call? I doubt they will give us much time for a drop off when they do call."

"Yes" Susan replied. "She told me she was able to do it by putting up some property as collateral for short term financing from some bank or other. Have you anything new to report as to my husband's death. Jessica made it very clear to me that we would need the insurance to be paid out in a timely manner to repay the borrowed money?"

"Unfortunately, no I have not. Rest assured that I am giving it my maximum attention.

"Gentlemen, Susan said aloud. "I have not had my evening swim since before, well you know, and I do miss it. Do you suppose it would be alright if I were to go to the beach for awhile this evening? I find it very relaxing and frankly, I could use some relaxation. I usually go to Bender's beach."

Oliver spoke up. "Absolutely mam, I'd be happy to drive you there. Mr. McCurdy perhaps you should accompany us? Just in case there may be some contact made to Susan's phone which she is to carry at all times.

"Of course, no problem, How about I meet you at the lounge at say 7 o'clock?

"Sounds good Mr. McCurdy, Thank you" Susan said.

Right on, everyone was catching on.

Oliver stood and escorted Susan to the door, very professionally of course. At least as professional as was possible for someone dressed like and organ grinders monkey.

I said good day, passed Olly the sporting goods store bag with the scanner in it, and closed the door. I gathered our paper, tore it into tiny shreds, and flushed the shreds down the toilet. It took a couple flushes to make sure they were gone.

CHAPTER

9

Oliver was punctual which is not necessarily the norm for him. I assumed it was because his new duties as chauffeur required some attention be paid to the time of day. Susan was dressed for a swim and the bikini she wore flattered her more than the expensive wardrobe she had worn earlier. I had worn some cut offs and a short sleeved flowered shirt that said tourist on the front just in case anyone was unsure of the weird attire. Oliver had donned some shorts and sandals but still wore his official chauffer uniform jacket with the bright gold shoulder straps and the monkey hat. The shorts and sandals complimented the organ grinder monkey look if that was the desired persona.

Initial greetings in the lounge were short lived as Susan declined any beverage and Oliver explained he was on duty and could not partake of alcoholic beverages. I supposed I was on duty as well and could live without the shot of rum

We proceeded to the beach area pausing momentarily after we had walked far enough to be away from any prying eyes while Oliver pulled the scanner from under his jacket and gave us all a quick scan. There were a couple surfers far out in the water but the beach was relatively unoccupied.

"All clear boss" he said. I do not know if he was addressing myself or Susan.

"Ok then we can speak confidentially" I said. "Yes boss, and this thing is great. You were right about the tracking device on the Mercedes, and also there were 3 bugs in Susan's home. One in the living room, one in the kitchen dining area, and one in the master bedroom. That was all of them and I was very thorough. I also checked for hidden cameras and stuff. The house has CC security cameras, but I could find none that monitored any of the interior of the home."

Susan spoke up. "I do not know who is listening or how these got installed but really feel like giving the fuckers something to listen to in the bedroom. I feel like I have been violated".

"I understand how that invasion of your privacy would piss you off, but it is best we hold off on that for the time being.

For the next while I have divided our task into three priorities. Susan, your safety is priority number 1. Oliver you are not to let Susan out of your sight other than in the bedroom or bathroom and then I think you should proceed her into any of these places to ensure they are secure from any outside intrusion, check the window and door locks etc. and then take up a position outside the door and stay there until Susan comes out."

What about sleep for me boss, or if I need the washroom? Oliver interjected. "Take a pillow and sleep outside Susan's door if you must, or don't sleep at all. If you need the washroom have Susan wait outside the door and do not lock it. Keep the grizzly stopper in one hand and use the other for whatever you need to do. It is your duty as a bodyguard and as a chauffer to see this is done" Oliver contemplated that. His look said it was contemplated with some disdain.

"Either that or you can get some adult diapers at a very affordable price if you would prefer."

A picture went through my mind of what Oliver would like in a diaper. It was rather horrifying so pushed it out of my mind.

Option two seemed to make option one more appealing to Oliver. "No worries boss, Susan will be safe with me twenty-four hours a day."

"Good Oliver, I know you are up to the task. Now priority number two, we need to get the extortionists paid off. I do not like to give in to their demands but we need to buy some time and get them off our backs so it will be a necessary evil. We will get that out of the way and then proceed to priority three which is to come up with some proof for the insurance company. Once the insurance money is paid to Susan, we can discuss our options to try and recover the money from the bad guys.

Ok, back to priority one Susan, your safety. We cannot at this time move you to a safe place. Not until after priority two, the bad guys are paid out the two million. I have made some arrangements for the moment after that happens. I have made arrangements to provide two clean rental vehicles untraceable back to any of our own names. Thank you to my dear mother, may she rest in peace, for not cancelling her credit card before or after she died."

"But boss," Olly started to say. I know what your thinking Olly, how would she cancel them after she died? I know it would be difficult and rest assured, once this case is passed, I will forward my Mother's new address to the credit card company and they can serve her notice of cancellation or collection at the Forest Lawn cemetery as they wish. My Mother was a firm believer in justice and would be more than happy to help in any way she could while she was alive, and I am simply fulfilling her wishes as I would have understood them to be. Bonus is, she does not have to wait for me to pay her back."

"Don't seem right boss" Olly said.

"Jesus Christ Olly, since when did you become the morality police? I started to rant but Susan ended speculation and the argument by suggesting we may be able to cover the credit card debt after insurance was collected.

"OK then, what we will do as soon as possible after the money drop, I will have a vehicle placed at a location where you can easily access it. It will have the keys in it, unless I have already given them to you, as well as some untraceable burner phones for each of you. I have also used the same credit card, *shut up Oliver*, to rent rooms in a hotel some distance away, the location of which I will reveal at a later time. It is extremely important that we continue with the ruse that we are unaware of the monitoring so that whoever it is that is monitoring us stays unaware that we are on to them. Having them think they know where we are and what we are thinking at all times is our ace in the hole which allows them to let their guard down and let us disappear from their surveillance.

"Good thinking boss, you are more cunning and conniving that I gave you credit for." Oliver was grinning.

"Kind of proud of myself too," I grinned back. "Now Susan, I know you think there are people you can trust but at this stage, only myself and Oliver are to be trusted, and in that regard, you must follow our instructions implicitly. Are you ok with that?"

"I honestly haven't felt this safe since I left Kansas, I put my fate in the capable hands you two gentlemen." Oliver's chest swelled with pride, and he patted the holster under his jacket grinning a little bit and nodding his head. I couldn't help but notice a slightly evil glint in his eyes.

"OK then gentlemen, may I go for a short swim while we are here? I am dressed for it and surely it is safe with you gentlemen looking out for me. You are welcome to join me if you wish." I scanned the beach for swimmers, wished I had brought a drink or two with me and said "Looks all clear to me, go ahead. I personally am not a big swimmer but if Oliver here will leave his jacket and hat behind, I'll be happy to look after them while you both go.

Oliver was a bit perplexed obviously wanting to go but concerned. "You can't touch my gun if I leave it here."

"Well, you can't take it with you, it would act as an anchor and drag you down until you drowned." I stated.

"Come on Oliver," Susan encouraged, "look we have the beach to ourselves, and we won't be long." She waved her arm toward the beach, kicked off her sandals and ran to the water. Oliver and I watched with much admiration as she ran into the water and executed a graceful dive once the water was deep enough. She surfaced and shouted back, "come on in, the waters fine" as she smiled and waved. I gave Olly a gentle tap on the shoulder, "go, you are neglecting your duties". He shucked off his chauffer attire and shirt and lumbered into the waves with all the grace of a drunken hippopotamus.

Susan was about 50 yards from shore and Oliver about half that distance when I turned to calculate the distance between myself and the lounge and contemplate making an effort to lug Oliver's chauffer attire and grizzly stopper to the lounge to fetch myself some liquid refreshment when I heard Susan shriek. My initial thought was a jelly fish sting, but I turned just in time to see her head disappear beneath the surface. The shriek was followed immediately by Olly's bellow which I would compare to a very angry hippopotamus if I knew what that sounded like. If a hippopotamus could do the 50-yard dash on the top of the water in 5 seconds that would describe Oliver's actions immediately after the bellow. He disappeared below the water in a splash displacing a volume of water significantly larger than his body mass called for, when he reached the point I had last seen Susan. Moments later Susan surfaced pulled from the water by Oliver's hand followed by someone with a snorkel and mask apparently grasping her ankle. I had dropped Oliver's clothing and was struggling to remove the oversized pistol from its holster when a crashing blow from Oliver's opposite hand served to dislodge the culprit's hand from Susan's ankle as well as the mask and snorkel from his head. I was not sure if the head stayed attached to the body or went with the snorkel. I didn't really care that much. I was just relieved to see Susan swimming quickly and gracefully towards the shoreline. I swear I could still hear Oliver bellowing even after he dived again below the surface. If Kraken or some other sea monster was down there, I suspected they were going to get an ass whipping from Oliver and pity the poor wearer of the snorkel. The water churned for a long enough time that I was becoming concerned for Oliver when he finally bobbed to surface. He was holding the snorkel and mask but I could not see any head attached to it. My relief seeing Susan swimming was short lived. A gun shot rang out. I did not see the bullet strike but did note that Susan had disappeared beneath the surface. As Oliver bellowed and charged toward Susan, I turned in the direction I thought the gun shot had originated. I noted movement on top of the cliff. May have been the shooter or may have been a confused fox or other innocent creature but I swung Oliver's cannon towards the movement and let fly with a couple of rounds. The noise was deafening. I would have to suggest to Oliver that he get a silencer for the damn thing. I kept one eye on the cliff for more movement as I checked to see if Oliver and Susan were ok. Oliver had Susan under one of his massive arms and was running for the cover of some rocky outcrops on the beach. I pounded one more round into the cliff to ensure the shooter knew I was still here, in a bad mood, and was not out of bullets if they wanted to play some more. People with guns think they are tough guys until you return fire then they usually re-evaluate their situation and, more often than not, run. I heard a vehicle start, tires squeal then the engine noise dissipated into the distance. I was not able to get a look at the vehicle. "Anybody hurt?" I shouted. Oliver had concealed Susan behind the rocks and was running towards me hollering "give me the gun boss". "Too late Olly, they are gone, is Susan ok?" I said. Oliver was panting, "She's fine boss, but whoever fired them shots won't be fine when I catch up to the fucker". He grabbed the gun in passing.

"Too late, Olly, I heard them leaving". "You sure" he called back. I am sure Oliver; I heard the cowardly bastards vehicle leaving. That cliff is two hundred feet high and unless you can fly, you are not going to make it up that way anyway. And besides that, you are neglecting your duty as a bodyguard. Let's get Susan to hell out of here before they come back for a rematch That was a high-powered rifle that fired the shot." He returned in a rushed lumbering fashion, still panting heading for the rock Susan was secured behind. With nothing but his wet shorts on, he did bear a striking resemblance to Shrek minus the green coloring. We approached the rock to find Susan quite unharmed. Excepting that one half of her upper bosom had escaped its confines either in the turmoil in the water or during the 50-yard dash under Olly's arm, she did not look to upset. Tough lady, And the escaped portion of her anatomy only enhanced my belief she was perfect to the core.

"Are you ok? I asked as we approached. "I'm sure they are gone". Oliver chimed in, "We will find those fuckers and they are going to find they made a big mistake attacking someone under my watch and will pay dearly for it, he paused, excuse my language." He was still panting, and their may have been small flames shooting out of his eyes. Susan stood, looking down and noticing she had an escapee, tucked it back into place. "I am fine, and I don't know what in the fuck is going on but whatever it is has pissed me off to no end and I will be more than happy to help hunt down those fuckers and let them know they fucked with the wrong lady", she paused, grinned, and said "Oliver, please excuse my language." Emphasis on my language.

Oliver grinned sheepish, or evil, maybe a combination. "I apologize mam for allowing you to be placed in distress." "Distress my ass, them fuckers were trying to kill me, and it certainly was not your fault. I should be apologizing for getting you guys into this whatever kind of goat fuck we got going on. I owe you my life Oliver and am very grateful for that".

Yes, she was beautiful when she was angry as well.

Oliver put on his monkey grinder hat and was squeezing into the matching jacket to get back into his chauffer mode. I was going to suggest we get the frail young lady out of there and she seemed to sense it. However, was not quite done her rant yet. I am getting a bit tired of this whole prissy, lady like bullshit. I can ride a horse, rope a steer, drive a tractor, kick the living shit out a of shit people like whoever got hold of my leg in the water, the sneaky bastard, and I can shoot a gun. Maybe not so great with a gun like yours Oliver but a 12-gauge shotgun will do me just fine for personal protection and I intend to get one very soon."

Both myself and Oliver were at a bit of a loss for words seeing this new side of Susan. We kept our mouth shut, and just gawked.

She pushed her wet hair back from her forehead and smiled. "Relax guys, have you never met a farmer's daughter before? I do not care who you are, how rich you are, or how tough you think you are; you don't fuck with a farmer's daughter. Let me see that gun of yours Oliver." Oliver passed it to her two-finger style like he was holding a stick of dynamite or maybe a snake. She took in her tiny hand and tried to get her fingers wrapped around the pistol grip. "Jeez, heavy thing. Weighs more than a shotgun", she said raising it in a two-handed shooting stance and sighting down the barrel. "Any chance that guy who had me by the leg may surface within range of this thing?"

Oliver picked up the snorkel and mask that he had somehow retained possession of as he transported Susan to the safety of the rocks. The face piece was shattered and the frame had a dent in it. Oliver looked at his knuckles which were scarred a bit.

"I am not sure, maybe not so good".

"Speaking of which" I said, did anybody get a good look at them, any idea who it was?"

"Not me, I had jus turned back to see where Oliver was and someone grabbed my leg and pulled me under. Took me by surprise and before I knew what was happening Oliver arrived and before I knew it I was back on surface of the water and heard what was either an elephant trumpeting, maybe calling to a mate, or Oliver telling me to swim. He seemed to have the situation well under control, so I done as instructed and headed for shore. About half-way back I heard the gunshot, saw the water splash just to my left so I dived and turned right. Next thing I knew I was in flight under Oliver's arm travelling at a frightening pace towards the rocks. Wow, you can move fast for a big guy Oliver." She smiled; he grinned his Shrek grin.

Thought he might say Aw, shucks, so before that happened, I said "Oliver, did you get a look at him?

"Not really boss, when I first got hold of him he had that mask on his face and of course he still had hold of Susan so as you often mention, things need to be done in priority fashion. First priority was getting him to unhand Susan so I gave him a shot of incentive right on the mask. I think I knocked it off," he looked at his knuckles again. Once Susan was on her way to safety, I went back under looking for him with every intention of showing him the proper way to ensure a person was drowned and all I could find was this". He held up the dented snorkel mask. "Then I heard the gunshot and my priority changed again to Susan's safety, which is my job as you know, and I think you saw the rest. About all I could say was that he was brown."

"Brown?" I queried.

"Yeah, you know, as in not black, not white, brown, maybe Mexican, or Indian, or middle eastern. Blood was red. At least I think it was his". He examined his knuckles again.

"Good, Oliver, that narrows it down to about 90 percent of the population of the planet earth. We should have him in no time."

Oliver had just started to remind me that I had also missed identifying a culprit who was not under the water which is rather more difficult to see through and the least I could have done was got a look at the vehicle when our battle of wits was interrupted by a siren and the flashing lights of a police cruiser driving through the barrier around the beach and proceeding directly towards us. Just as well. I had time to state that I do not enjoy engaging in a battle of wits with an unarmed man to Olly without giving him time for a come back.

Great. It was my good friend officer Morgan.

"Well, well, well," he said, exiting the vehicle.

"I get a report of shots fired, and who do I find but Shits and giggles, **in person**. Why does that not surprise me McCurdy? By the way, which of you is shits and which is giggles? I have never been able to figure that out for sure." No one responded to his query. I could think of no response other than that perhaps he should not waste time thinking about that while he was still trying figure out whether his ass hole had been punched or bored, but let good sense override my instincts. Oliver kept his jaw clenched which both surprised and worried me. He was still pumped full of adrenaline and itching to drown someone. Morgan was a good candidate but drowning him in his uniform would not only waste a good uniform but may cause strife with the department which we did not need.

"So, McCurdy, tell me your bullshit." He leaned back against his car.

"Well officer Morgan, this may be a bit of a stretch to believe but swear it is exactly as I was able to comprehend the facts at the time, but what happened was, my colleague Oliver and Susan had gone into the water for a nice swim. I stayed on shore to guard their belongings as we all know the high crime rate in this jurisdiction and the tardy response of the police department, no reflection on yourself of course.

Something grabbed hold of Susan's ankle, may have been Kraken, or a giant squid or octopus, we cannot be sure as we never actually seen what it was, and started pulling her under. Mr. Barnett rushed to her aid and was able to free her ankle from the beast so she could escape. Some good Samaritan up on the bank may have seen what it was and fired at it with a high-powered rifle. As Mr. Barnett and Ms. Harcourt made for the safety of the rocks over there, I took a cue from the good Samaritan and fired a couple rounds as well into the area I suspected the beast may be lurking, to buy some time for them to reach safety. I am sorry we can't be of more help with the description of the beast however you may want to notify the coastguard that there is something fierce lurking in their waters."

Morgan waited momentarily then spit, then spoke. "Uh huh, I see. Sea monsters eh? And tell me, was this sea monster wearing that snorkel and mask", he nodded towards Oliver still holding the broken, dented face mask.

Oliver looked down, with surprise as though just noticing it was still in his hand. "Uh, no sir, I found that after Susan was freed from it's grasp. I'm thinking it may have upchucked the remnants of its last meal when I clobbered it trying to entice it to let go of Susan's leg." Oliver produced a very good rendition of Shrek's innocent grin. Susan had turned away straining to contain her laughter.

Morgan sighed and leaned off the vehicle. "Jesus Christ McCurdy, you need to change your name to bull shits and giggles incorporated. You understand I do have to file a report on this and be damned if I am going to mention any sea monsters. So, I guess my investigation has revealed that McCurdy and company were found on the beach apparently under the influence of some illicit hallucinogenic drugs possibly combined with alcohol." He opened the door to his cruiser and offered his usual departure valediction combined with a bit of advice, "Fuck off McCurdy, and for the safety of all of you, please be advised you may be in over your head and in danger of grievous harm. And not from any fucking sea monsters."

"Thank you for your concern for our welfare and for your prompt response. By the way, Officer Morgan, do you carry an assault rifle in your cruiser? Just curious", I said.

"None of your fucking business, and once again, Fuck off McCurdy. Excuse my language mam, he turned towards Susan. "Conversing with Mr. McCurdy tends to make me forgetful of the social graces."

"Thank you again for your concern sir" I said.

As he put his cruiser in gear and drove off, Oliver waved bye, bye. He received a middle finger response from Morgan's hand extended out the out the driver's side window.

I was relatively certain the excitement on the beach was over for the day. My brain was still trying to sort out who the bad guys were and what the relationships were, if any, between them. One thing was certain. I had just witnessed an organized attempt on Susan's life, and possibly mine and Oliver's as well. It was unfortunate that Oliver had lost his grip on the snorkeling guy. Alive I could have enjoyed watching Oliver, or maybe the new side of Susan's personality beat some information out of them or, even if Oliver had drowned them which is the much more likely case, could have gotten a look at them and maybe Susan could have identified them. So far, our investigation had revealed more questions than answers. Was Dustin Harcourt even dead? I hoped so, as alive he would throw a wrench into our cushy percentage arrangement, however I was becoming less certain all the time. Were the Jackals the only bad guys and if so, why would they try to kill Susan who was their only hope for payment. That made no sense. And what was Morgan or the police forces involvement or was it just Morgan's normal incompetence which due to past experiences, I considered to have no limits. I may have to reassess that opinion. He had been after my ass since the first time I had made him look stupid which was not difficult to do. The timing of his arrival was such that he could have fired at Susan, and the aforementioned incompetence would account for the miss.

And why had wonderful Jessica hired McCurdy and not some company with more resources. I was beginning to believe her glowing reference had come from her miss-perceived assumption that we may not be all that competent in addition to being susceptible to sale of our integrity.

Priority one remained to be Susan's safety. Were the Jackals lone wolves with a legitimate claim to a debt, or rather a legitimate claim to an illegitimate debt might be more like it or, was it a collaboration between two parties or all parties? WTF was going on?

The immediate concern was where would Susan be safe until we could pay out the assumed Jackals debt and move them out of the picture. Giving in to blackmailer's demands was rarely a good idea. They tended to come back to the well if they knew there was water still to be had but two million bucks might hold them off for awhile. We could look at recovery at a later time. I was wondering why we had not heard from them yet. Until that happened, it was agreed that we had little choice but to maintain the status quo knowing that we were being monitored and keep up the pretense of being unaware and incompetent when we were actually aware we were being listened to with one exception. I referenced our evasive action plan. I made arrangements to rent a vehicle. I would park my vehicle with the transponder in it at my office and sneak away from my office / sleeping quarters and take up a position near Susan's home where I could monitor the exterior of the building and be prepared should some action be required to thwart any future attempts on Susan's life. I had great confidence in Olie but he could tend to be a bit aggressive and focus on killing any perceived threats forgetting the end goal of keeping Susan, and our financial arrangement with her safe. We headed back to the parking lot to retrieve our vehicles. We walked past the lounge much to my dismay. My daily rum allotment was being seriously neglected. I hoped I could live through the current investigation and make it up. Right now, I gave myself a 50-50 chance of that.

CHAPTER 10

I returned to my office with the vehicle that some unknown person, or more likely persons was monitoring the location of. I had informed Oliver and Susan that I would be driving a nondescript rental vehicle, a grey Chev Malibu, and would be monitoring Susan's residence over the night, so please Oliver, do not shoot anyone in the described vehicle, or the vehicle itself. As an added precaution I had paid a bit extra for no fault insurance on the car. Or rather, my departed Mother's credit card had purchased the extra insurance. Mother would be proud of her son for taking extra precautions.

I had a nourishing snack of leftover Chinese food, washed it down with my last half of a shot of rum as a proactive medicinal gesture to destroy any bacteria that may have been forming on the leftovers for however many days they had been sitting on the counter, waited an appropriate length of time, and shut off the lights so any observers would assume I had retired to my sofa and gone to sleep.

Feeling extremely clever and devious, I stealthily moved on all fours to peak out the windows to check if there were anything of note out of place, such as a thug or two sitting in a vehicle watching my office / apartment. There was a police cruiser parked on the street but most likely just some of our boys in blue looking for a late-night snack. It did not appear to be occupied.

I still had not sorted out who the bad guys were and was a bit confused how officer Morgan may know that we could be in grave danger, so I tucked the little gun Oliver had expended considerable social graces and a few bullets retrieving and exited the office through the fire escape / stairs from the backdoor to the first-floor landing which also served as access to the kitchen area of the Chinese restaurant. There was a sign on the door that said FIRE ESCAPE emergency use only- alarm will sound, but I knew that it had either been broken for years or was just a sign to deter traffic on the stairs and divert potential customers to the restaurant. I peered out the window to check the back alley before opening the exit door. Nothing of note there. Damn I was good at being clever and sneaky is what I was thinking when the face seemingly materialized out of the darkness in front of me. It was not a friendly face. Scruffy whiskers, unwashed the past year at the least, and the smile was far from friendly. The knife he was holding up and pointing at my face indicated to me that this was not a friendly greeting.

"Fuck" I said, "I don't have time for this shit."

"Give me all your fucking money" he said, much louder than our close quarters required.

"You know", I calmly said, "that intelligent people can communicate without shouting or swearing."

"Give me your fucking money" he said, a bit louder and waved the knife in my face for emphasis.

"No, I shouted back, "You give me all your fucking money" as I pulled the little gun out of my pocket and stuck it in his face.

Although not as formidable looking as Oliver's grizzly stopper, it had the desired effect. He backed off a bit, still waving the knife in front of himself.

He stuttered a bit something about having no money, I assume at a loss for words, then I guess he felt committed to be all macho and lunged toward me with the knife.

I sidestepped and as he was passing whacked him on the side of the head with the revolver. He dropped like a sack of hammers, face down in the dirt.

My right foot was in the locked and loaded position in case he needed a little more encouragement from my boot to stay asleep but there was no need.

His head obviously had less tolerance for sudden impacts than Oliver's. He was out like a light.

I looked around to make sure I didn't have an audience. To be on the safe side, I thought I better check for Id and see who the dumbass was just in case he was somehow affiliated with the bad guys, whoever they were.

I kicked the knife a few feet away from his hand, checked his back pockets, then rolled him over checked the front pockets and his jacket. He had no Id, and he had no money either. He did have half a mickey of rum in his jacket pocket. The missing top half of the mickey may have accounted for his clumsiness and his bravado. I rolled him into the recovery position I had learned in numerous first aid courses, put the rum in my pocket, and left.

Pissed me off. Fucking city. A person not safe in their own damn backyard. Granted, my backyard was not exactly in the suburbs.

I continued my quest to make my way to the parking lot a few blocks away where I had gotten the rental car delivered to, detouring to the open street long enough to use a payphone and report a guy who may need assistance behind the restaurant.

The Malibu was there as requested, with the keys hidden inside the gas tank cover, also as requested.

Traffic was light this time of day and I made my way to Susan's residents in good time, making up a bit of what I lost dealing with the stupid damn mugger.

Her home was in a much better area of the city where you would not expect to find a mugger in your back yard. Not a good neighborhood for Oliver and his cannon to be stationed. Hopefully the neighbors did not have any cats that may interrupt his sleep.

The outside the house looked luxurious, but not extravagant compared to the neighboring residences. Situated on a large lot with a half moon paved driveway with two entrance / exits located about 300 feet apart which indicated a lot size likely in the 500 x 500-feet square range. The house was

3 tiered, probably about 7- 8000 sq feet not including the attached two car garage. I done a surveillance lap around the block noting my escape routes should they be needed. The front yard was enclosed by a manicured hedge about 5 feet high, the driveway entrance and exits were ungated indicating a low crime rate. The backyard was enclosed by a white board fence also about 5 feet high on 3 sides, a deck and the obligatory swimming pool closes to the house leaving some lawn, then some space for a little extra parking in the rear. A typical home in a typical affluent neighborhood.

Many homes had visible CCTV security however as far as I could tell, Susan's either did not or was much better hidden. I done a couple extra laps around the block and noted nothing out of the ordinary so

parked the car down the block on the opposite side of the street far enough away as to look as though I was may have been visiting at another residence and prepared for a long night of nothing to see. Surveillance can be incredibly boring. It can also be punctuated by chaos and pandemonium at any given moment. I had brought my little kit of disguises with me, notably a blond hippy length wig and thought about taking a walk through some of the shrubbery to stay alert however I expected I would encounter some motion detected lighting that may be hard to explain at one am. At 1:30 am I was about to nod off when a vehicle entered travelling towards me. I slunk down in the seat to make the vehicle look empty. The vehicle passed very slowly. As it passed, I raised my head enough to get a peak at the vehicle and tried to get the licence number by looking in my mirror to no avail. I could tell it was a late model Lexus which fit the neighborhood and odds were, it was some businessman making his way home from a nightclub or maybe a strip joint. I discounted that idea when it made its second lap around the block. That got my spider senses tingling and served to shake any thoughts of sleep from my mind and put me into high alert mode. I was positioned myself so I could get a visual of the licence plate on the next lap, but the next lap never came. I was about to make a lap myself to see where the vehicle had gone when the light in Susan's back yard came on. Assuming it was a motion detector which turned the light on, I quickly donned my disguise and left the vehicle, running to the hedge where I could make my way to the backyard undetected. I was just arriving at the point where hedge meets backyard fence when I heard a familiar rhinoceros bellow, followed by a splash. I forced my way through the shrubbery to the yard to note Oliver in the swimming pool, quite clearly in the process of drowning someone. Drowned until they are dead people cannot talk so with total disregard for my apparel or the fact that I cannot swim, I bailed into the pool to assist in the capture of the trespasser while he was still alive for interrogation. Upon arrival in the pool, I heard another bellow and found myself submerged and unable to breathe. Had my head been above water, I still could not have breathed until the two huge paws that had my windpipe squeeze shut let go. I was struggling to free myself, when even from below the water, I heard the unmistakeable roar of Oliver's grizzly stopper.

It must have startled Olly temporarily as well, as the grip on my windpipe eased and I could feel the wig being pulled from my head. I grabbed Oliver's arm and pulled myself up until my head came out of the water and gasped in a couple breaths of air.

"What the fuck?" Oliver said, holding my wig in his outstretched arm, which I was holding on to, to keep from drowning.

I could not yet speak but I was well enough to know I had much to say.

"What the fuck?", Oliver repeated, then seemingly realizing it was me was holding onto his arm, paused and said, "boss, what the fuck are you doing in the deep end of the pool? You know you can't swim."

"No shit Oliver, "I gasped, "now get me out of the fucking pool."

Oliver dragged me to the edge and I was struggled up onto the deck, still gasping, trying to get my windpipe to expand to its normal size. My eyes were working ok and took in my surroundings. Oliver bobbing in the pool, Susan standing in the open patio door wearing a short, short nightgown, holding Oliver's cannon. She winked and blew over the top of the barrel. No trespasser to be seen, but I did hear the distant squeal of tires cornering to fast not to great a distance away indicating he was gone and, in a hurry, to be gone.

I was getting my voice back and it was my turn. "What the fuck Oliver, You, just tried to kill me" I squeaked through my bruised vocal chords.

"Yeah, uh, sorry boss, I didn't know it was you," he said sheepishly glancing at my dripping blond hippy wig in his hand, then added "What are you doing out here all dressed up in drag?"

"Fucking, fuck", my voice was getting louder. "Shit a Goddamn, excuse my language," I coughed, remembering there was a lady present. Albeit a lady holding a smoking 45 caliber pistol may not have been offended by my language.

"And" I panted, struggling to stand, "while you were trying to kill me you let the bad guy get away for Christ sakes."

"Geez, calm down boss, you're going to give yourself a heart attack or a stroke or a hernia or something. Here, let me help you to a chair where you can relax and get your breath back" he offered as he reached under me with one massive arm and half carried, half dragged me to the deck and plopped me into a chair.

I breathed for a few moments then quietly in as condescending a manner as I could manage, I said, "It is called a disguise, Oliver, I was going incognito, dumbass, as in private investigator stuff, understand? Like, trying to be secretive, sneaky may be a word you would better comprehend. Surveillance sometimes requires that you do not let the other person, or persons in this case whom we do not yet know who they are, only that they wish to cause our client and ourselves grievous harm, do not know who you are."

Oliver was doing his best to look as though he understood that he was receiving a serious reprimand, looking down, bottom lip protruding in a pout, until he placed the sopping wet wig on his block head and said, "I get it boss, no one would ever recognize me now", he smiled, or more like showed his teeth, perhaps not intentionally mocking me but doing a very good job of it never the less. He had a point. He just looked like a funny colored Shrek with a blond wig on his block.

"You make a piss poor hippy" I said. "if you wish to be unrecognized you may want to try a gorilla costume or put on some camouflage clothes and pretend you are a tree or a tank, something a little less feminine. He looked so stupid standing there in moose size wet boxer shorts with a wet blond wig on his head, I had to smile. "No, no, I've got it wrong Olly. The wig is perfect, all you need is a ballerina dress to go with it" I giggled.

"Boss, if I didn't know better, I would think that was sarcasm. It hurts my feelings that you are unable to see my feminine side."

"My friend, a platoon of psychiatrists with all the tools of torture could not find you feminine side, and that is not sarcasm, that is just a fact."

Susan was still leaning in the doorway with the cannon watching our battle of wits unfazed by the fact that someone may have just tried to kill her again looking rather amused by it all.

"Are you boys done your little squabble now?' She sounded very motherly, and she was holding a 45 which she obviously knew how to use, which brought us back to the moment and the realization we surely had better things to consider.

"We're good Susan. He just called me friend." Oliver stated putting his arm around my shoulders and giving a bit of a hug. "He just gets a little worked up like this when anyone tries to kill him, not just me. People try to kill him on a regular basis, and it always makes him angry. An unavoidable occupational hazard of his chosen profession. He needs to get his anger under control, take some anger management classes, maybe learn to meditate like I do to help him mellow out."

That statement coming out of Oliver just dumbfounded me. I could only shake my head and try to express my confusion with WTF hand gestures. Christ, I was losing a battle of wits to an unarmed man.

Susan was still leaning in the doorway, grinning now.

I roughly shrugged Olly's arm off my shoulders and stood. "Good to see you boys have made up" Susan said. "Yeah, yeah", I give Oliver a shove to show my manliness and ripped my wig out of his hand.

"If you boys are over your little tiff, I would suggest you come inside and dry off, there is a bit of a chill in the air" she said, as she pushed herself up from leaning on the patio doors and turned to go inside. She put her finger to lips in a "stay quiet gesture" and wiggled her finger to indicate we should follow.

Oliver and I followed obediently. It felt a bit strange to see the shy lady I'd met only a few days ago turn into the take charge person she was being now. We followed her into what I assumed was a library and closed the door behind us. She set the revolver on a desk and took a seat behind it motioning us to be seated on the available chairs in front. "Oliver has swept the room for any listening devices, and I am confident no one is listening to us in here.

This is really starting to piss me off" she stated matter-of-factly.

Olly and I sat dutifully as instructed, I guess like boys who had been misbehaving.

Susan was right. We had serious business to tend to. I would deal with dumbass's insubordination later.

I cleared my throat, and tried to gain control of the conversation, and the situation.

"Ok, so, thanks to my esteemed colleague, and maybe myself, we have no idea who was lurking in your yard with what we must assume were nefarious intentions. We blew our chance to catch and interrogate the culprit, once again, I glared at Ollie, and also did not get a licence plate number or even a good description of the vehicle although I am pretty sure it was the Lexus I seen earlier while I was in my car." Susan interrupted, "Well, I am pretty sure if you find the vehicle it will have a bullet hole somewhere near the passenger's door, or maybe the rear door on the passenger side, it was moving when I fired so I can't be positive. And it was a dark colored car, black I think, or maybe very dark brown or grey."

Oliver added, "and the guy was not one of the Bobbsey twins. Head was not big enough," he clarified.

"Ok, I said, so we are looking for a dark colored car with a bullet hole in the passenger's side, driven by someone with a small head". "Not small boss, just normal size, Bobbsey twins head are bigger than normal" Oliver noted.

"Well, the bullet hole might stand out, but I do not expect we will ever see that vehicle again. Probably hidden by now, getting a little body work to patch the hole. I hope my cover wasn't blown, I added." "No way boss, If I couldn't recognize you in that wig, no one could, although I may have been a bit preoccupied when you arrived" Oliver stated.

"Thanks for the vote of confidence Oliver, but I still need to get back to my rental car. I doubt anyone will be back to bother you tonight, unless, that is, we got to a bug in the house where they can hear us and say something to convince them that it is safe to come back and finish their dirty work".

"Not a good idea boss, Oliver stated, if they come back with more firepower, we don't have anything to hold them off other than my one grizzly stopper. These guys are a scary bunch and they won't stop. That is two obvious attempts on Susan's life and I am sure they will keep trying"

That gave me pause to think. "You are probably right Oliver, we need to beef up our firepower. I am just wondering if it is safe for Susan to stay here with just you and the grizzly stopper tonight."

Susan stood from her chair and leaned on the desk. "I am not running away from my home, case closed. Yes I understand there is someone out there who seems to very badly wants me dead and I assume it has something to do with a 10 million dollar life insurance policy. The Jackals or whoever looking for the two million would have no reason to want me dead at least until they get their money, and I am still carrying that burner phone 24 hours a day waiting for them to call. Jessica called earlier and said the money was ready for pick up from the office safe. As soon as they call me, I am ready to deliver it. Besides, I will not take this gong show back to my family so where the hell could I go that would be safer than right here with the two gentlemen who have foiled the first two attempts on my life". She winked at Oliver. Oliver's face turned to mush, and his chest puffed up like Yosemite Sam. He blubbered something incoherent.

I took a few seconds to absorb that. She was right too, and I wasn't about to say she could maybe have more qualified bodyguards.

"You are the boss Susan, and Oliver, I am impressed that you have the logical function of your brain working. You are starting to think like a private investigator."

"I'm learning from the best boss", he smirked.

'Stop sucking up, don't forget you just tried to drown the best, and besides, it just does not look good on you. Grovelling is not your forte."

I stood and put the blond wig on my head, "Ok then, I am out of here. I passed my little gun to Susan. I can find my own way out. I will return to my car the way I came in." Oliver gave me a half assed salute, and Susan smiled and waved bye-bye with the little pistol. "And, let me know the instant you get a call from the Jackals. Not sure how we will handle that. We will just have to wing it I suppose."

I made my way outside and back to my rental. Much to my relief, it was an uneventful trip. I got into the car, removed my wig, and headed back to the office / home to get a little shut eye. That too was uneventful until I was out of the cul-de-sac and about 4 blocks from Susan's house. I could see the flashing red and blue lights, along with some orange tow truck lights indicating there had been an accident. The tow truck was blocking the road winching a vehicle out of the ditch as I slowed my approach. I stopped behind the police car as instructed by the officer motioning with his hand to wait. I recognized the voice when he called out, "we won't be long, just s few minutes." The voice that I recognized, recognized my face and turned back for a second look. He put his hand down and walked back to my driver's side window. Ah, fuck, I thought. It is late and I am tired. I rolled the window down. "Well, well", Sergeant Morgan said, "if it isn't my favorite private dick, or maybe just my favorite dickhead, McCurdy from the esteemed firm of shits and giggles investigations. Why am I not surprised to find you out this late at night very near to the scene of a rather suspicious accident. A witness called it in, and I arrive to find not a soul around. The witness says two great big tough looking guys in some kind of monster truck with huge tires pulled up beside this gentleman in a rental car and just rammed one big tire into him and knocked him off the road. Then the monster truck squealed to a stop and one big fat bald guy with stringy hair got out of the truck and took a couple pot shots at the driver, whom, I guess must be still running seeing as we can't find a body down there. Too bad the witness didn't hang around. I guess the gunfire maybe discouraged that, as well as discouraged him from giving his name. Called it in anonymously. Even decent people do not want to get involved sometimes.

I arrive and guess who the only vehicle to come by here tonight is. "You," he poked me in the shoulder for emphasis. You wouldn't happen to know any big guys that drive a monster truck, run people off the road and shoot ats people, do you?

"Damn redneck teenagers I would suspect," I shook my head.

"Maybe it is just my suspicious nature, but again McCurdy, he repositioned himself, I suspect that you may not be telling me the whole truth. It is four in the morning and you are not drunk which indicates to me that you must be on a serious business outing. There is that he shifted again changing his angle of lean on my car, and there is also the fact I had to attend a previous complaint from a highly respectable gentleman in the parking lot outside a restaurant that just happens to be located right directly below your office facilities. The guy says that some thug held him up with a gun, stole his money and his rum, then gave him a pistol whipping upside the head leaving him for dead. Said if he wasn't so physically fit, he would probably be dead now. You do not know anything about that either I do not suppose?" I did not respond. After a moment he went on."

Do you have any weapons on you? Or… any rum on you? My victim gave a very good description of the rum. Not real good description of the perpetrator other than he looked like a long-haired blond asshole. The asshole part fits your description, but not so much the blond unless your serious business this evening was with a hairdresser.

"No sir, I said, and as you have so correctly deduced, I have been engaged in a serious business outing so unfortunately was not by my office there to assist the poor guy", I replied.

"Hmmm," Morgan scowled. "I know which one of you is shits and which one is giggles now. You are so full of shit, the name sticks to you just like shit". I can't get any sleep without a fuckup going on someplace and when I attend to the fuckup I find some involvement of Mr. Shits of shits and giggles investigations. Sounds like a might to many coincidences going on.

I let the shits and giggles comments slide. I'd lost a battle of wits with Oliver tonight so was not functioning at me best, my ass was dragging, and I preferred to keep my socializing with those who protect and serve and bad mouth me to a minimum.

The tow truck had the tail end of the vehicle up on the road now and I couldn't help but notice it was a late model dark colored 4 door Lexus sedan with a quite noticeable hole about an inch in diameter right about where the post is between the front and rear doors. A small sticker on the rear window identified it as an Avis rental. That solved the mystery of where our perpetrators vehicle was but added the mystery of who the hell was driving the monster truck that had run it off the road, and why did they do that. Jealous of the competition to kill Susan? This shit didn't make sense. How many people wanted to kill a sweet Midwest farmer's daughter?

Morgan had noticed my interest in the vehicle.

"Yes Mr. shits, he said, that does look like a bullet hole. Strange thing is, there is an almost matching hole on the other side. And yet our witness only mentioned one shot being fired and as it was being fired from the highway, that shot would have been aimed at the driver's side of the car.

What does that suggest to your superior deductive capabilities McCurdy?

He paused, I assumed waiting for a reply. He had gone from Mr. Shits to McCurdy indicating the possibility that he may actually be requesting an opinion.

"Well sir, my limited observations would indicate a couple of things.

One, the driver of the car is not a patriotic American as indicated by the brand name of the vehicle being of a type not made in north America. Two, it is a rental vehicle which indicates the driver is not local to the area, most likely arrived by air to the airport where he picked up the vehicle, and I would surmise that you will find the rental is most likely to be under a false name. That leaves open the possibility that the driver of the vehicle is of questionable character, possibly even lives offshore somewhere and may not be the innocent victim we perceive him to be at this juncture of the investigation.

The monster truck occupants are likely to be local or at least American and likely to a little bit redneck. Redneck Americans are noted to be very patriotic people. As for the bullet holes on both sides of the vehicle, I could only suggest there must have been an armed third party waiting in the bushes off the road, who fired at exactly the same moment as the guy who took a pot shot after running the vehicle into the ditch. The only possible conclusive point I could arrive at given the limited evidence is that you should only drive made in America vehicles in this town and to do otherwise may be hazardous.

"Hmph, Morgan grunted. As always Mr. Shits, your input is sincerely appreciated and as always Mr. Shits, it is total bullshit."

He slapped the door of my made in America malibu as the tow truck pulled out of the way opening my lane. "Fuck off McCurdy"

"Thank you sir and thank you for your dedication to the people's safety in our community regardless of the time of day."

I put the car in gear and fucked off as instructed while Morgan gave me the finger behind his back.

CHAPTER

11

Morgan had managed to waste enough of my time that the stores would soon be opening so I dropped off my rental car at the location I had selected and walked back to the office to pick up my car with the location transmitter attached. I stopped by the only long enough toto make sure anyone listening would think I had just gotten out of bed. Taking the Mercedes I drove to the shopping mall, parked in the lot on side of the building, went inside, purchased a large sport gear bag, and called a cab to meet at the opposite doors of the mall. I got in the cab and gave him the address of address of a merchant I had dealt with before, Eagle Arms corporation whom I knew would have a good stock to beef up the weaponry as I had discussed with Oliver. It was still early so I had the cab drop me off at a restaurant within walking distance of my destination for some breakfast. My body was still functioning on the well aged leftovers from the night before. I would use the time while having my bacon and eggs to do some contemplating on my case.

I sipped my black double extra large coffee and considered.

There was more than one player in the game for sure that seemed intent on the demise of my client, or maybe not. I was pretty sure the Jackals angle was correct, but they only wanted money which was probably owed to them by Harcourt. Regardless of the questionable reasons for the debt but killing my client before they had collected the debt, or even after would be counter productive. Dead people tend to care very little about any earthly debts and are not very good package delivery drivers. If left alive, they could always go back to the well for another bucket of money in the future if the opportunity, or necessity presented itself. If she were dead, that well was dry.

My spider senses had been tingling about Jessica ever since she had given me the glowing reference and not much had happened to change that. Granted she had sourced the 2 million bucks and had it ready in cash which was no small feat. Maybe I had misjudged her, but if she was not involved then who was the party who had made two attempts on Susan's life? Maybe there were two factions of the Jackals trying to be first to collect the debt, or one faction not wanting her to pay up. That was a dumb ass thought that made absolutely no sense to me but neither did anything else.

Who would stand to benefit from Susan's demise? That was the question I had to answer.

I finished my breakfast and walked over to Eagle arms to check his inventory. I picked out a 38 special revolver and then checked out his other firepower. Susan had mentioned she was adept with a shotgun so I was browsing when the owner approached to offer assistance. "Hey McCurdy, he greeted, what you looking at shotguns for? Are you going duck hunting? He smirked. "Goose", I said.

He pulled a 12-gauge Remington model 870 tactical pump action shotgun off the rack and passed it to me. "These are popular with all the goose hunters, light weight, smooth action, will take magnum shells if you wish, take the plug out of the magazine and it holds 5 shells including the one in the chamber if that happens to be legal in your jurisdiction. I know the legalities would be very important to you," more smirking before he went on, "A very versatile weapon that may come in handy for other events in the business you are in. Just so you can make use of it outside of hunting season, he grinned again.

I pumped the action. It was smooth. "Ok I said, this should suffice. Do you have three? Do you have cash he asked? As a matter of fact, I do, I said. "Well then yes, I most certainly do have three, meet you at the till" he headed into the back to get two more.

He returned to the till and started ringing up my bill. I put the sport bag on the counter and said, "won't be needing the boxes they came in, just put them in here." "Not a problem, these are also very durable and a couple scratches won't hurt the functioning at all. Will there be anything else sir? Perhaps some ammunition?"

"Yes please, give me 3 boxes of 25, 12-gauge buckshot shells, about 8 shot per shell, and 3 boxes of 25, rifled slugs."

"Yes sir, that is what most goose hunters choose for shot" he laughed. "Them gooses in big trouble"

"Oh", I added, "better give me a box of about number 4 lead shot as well." He was as smart as Morgan and knew the buckshot and slugs ammunitions were not made for goose hunting and that I was full of bullshit. Both were designed for big game but traditionally buckshot was for people, and slugs were for nothing smaller than a grizzly bear at close range. "Going goose hunting in grizzly country" I explained to no avail. He placed the shotguns and ammunition in the bag, still grinning like the Cheshire cat.

"There you go McCurdy; I will watch the news to see how your hunting trip is going". He laughed out loud.

I called a cab and lugged my sports bag outside to wait.

When the cab arrived, I loaded sports bag full of goodies and had the cab driver return me to the mall where I retraced my route back through the shopping mall and out the opposite door. I drove past the sot where I had left the checking to make sure no one had stolen the #2 un-bugged rental car I had parked in the lot in preparation for moving Susan to a safe place that had no listening devices planted. I done a quick check of the rental to make sure no tracking devices had been attached. Nothing obvious but to be safe I would bring back the scanner and double check if I had time.

The damn bag was heavy so I drove the Mercedes back past my stashed rental and locked the gear bag in the trunk, then returned the Mercedes to the front of my office and went inside hoping I could catch a couple winks. It was day 3 and the time limit provided by the Jackals for delivery of the 2 million was getting close to expiring so I expected Susan would hear from them soon.

I climbed the stairs to my office, went inside and bypassed my desk on the way to my bed, stopping at the washroom on the way. I looked in the mirror, and sure enough, I looked like shit. Maybe Morgan was on to something. I thought it was only an exceedance of my rum capacity that made my eyes puff out and gain red fracture lines through them but apparently lack of sleep had a similar effect. I splashed a little water on my face and headed for my bed. When I removed my jacket and tossed it on a chair, the thump made me recall the bottle of ill-gotten rum in the pocket. Well, I thought, just one little shot and then a nap.

Alas, it was not to be. The burner phone in my pocket I had purchased for communication with Oliver vibrated.

CHAPTER

12

I answered. "It is show time boss", Oliver said.

"Forget the dramatics Oliver, what was the instruction?"

"Have the money, in cash, one-hundred-dollar unmarked bills, in a plain duffel bag ready to go within the hour and wait for another call for further instructions. Susan has called Jessica to make sure the money is ready. Jessica said she has the money and we can meet her at Harcourt holdings building to take it out of the safe and give it to her."

Any other instructions? "Just one boss, for Susan to come alone."

"Shit, I was afraid of that" "No worries, Boss, I got it covered. Me and grizzly stopper are already climbing into the trunk of her car. Susan and I have small two-way radios for communication. She will push the transmit button so I can listen to any calls. I will try to text you any important information from my cell phone."

"Good job Oliver", and I will be tailing you in my rental car from the time you pick up the money at Harcourt's building. Whatever happens, do not get separated from Susan"

"No worries boss". I heard the "thunk" of the trunk lid close as Oliver disconnected the call.

Even a spacious Mercedes trunk would be a tight fit for someone the size of Oliver. I wondered how he could text with thumbs and fingers the size of beef sausages.

I bounded down the backstairs out the exit on the way to where I had left my untracked rental. I slammed the push bar on the exit door, felt a thump, and arrived outside just in time to see my previous acquaintance, the failed mugger guy, roll down the steps backwards and bash his head on the parking lot pavement. I didn't have time for this shit but paused long enough to make sure he was going to get up.

He rolled over, looked at me groggily and slurred "You're the guy who stole my whiskey"

"It wasn't whiskey dumb ass, it was rum, and you owed me that for not killing you". He was going to live so I carried on without waiting for a reply.

I ran to the location of my rental car. On arrival I moved the duffle bag with my newly purchased weaponry from the trunk to the back seat of the car, removed one shotgun from the bag, removed the plug from the magazine allowing me to load four 2 ¾ inch double OT buckshot shells plus one in the chamber giving me 5 shots before reloading, and placed it in the front seat with me.

It took less than 15 minutes for me to travel the distance to Harcourt holdings office building. Susan's car was the lone vehicle in the public parking lot in front of the building. I kept moving and circled the block to stay out of sight until Susans car left. I noted a nearly identical to Susan's Mercedes in the back of the building inside an enclosed fence which said Harcourt holdings employee parking only. I assumed that would be Jessica Baird's car and she would be inside transferring the cash from the safe to Susan's possession.

I also noted a late model 4x4 pickup that was all decked out to say "Redneck" with flood lights on the headache rack and fog lights on the front bumper about 2 blocks down from the Harcourt office building. I was quite certain it was just a coincidence but tucked it away in the corner of my mind for future reference. A lifetime in this business had honed my observational skills,

On my third lap around the block Susan's car pulled out and I followed trying to stay far enough behind so as to stay inconspicuous.

My radio crackled. "Boss, instruction are to follow the coast highway north and wait for more instructions."

"Got it Olly" I replied.

That was good. It allowed me to stay far out of site and speed to the destination as required. I slowed to the speed limit. Traffic was not heavy but there was enough that my little malibu rental would not be noticed. I made sure I had rented vehicles with no identifying marks like Hertz rental or anything on them.

I was about to speed up a bit to keep Susan's taillights within site when a black Mercedes with blacked out windows went speeding past me. What the fuck? How many black Mercedes were there in this town? My spider senses started to tingle. I sped up a little but stayed a quarter mile or so behind the redneck's dream truck.

My radio crackled "New instruction boss, Susan supposed to throw case with the money over the bank right where her hubby flew over the cliff.

That was not that far away. I pinned it. I could see a party starting soon and didn't want to be late.

"Tell Susan as soon as you can not to get out of the vehicle if she can help it. Throw the case out the window over the bank if that is possible.

I rounded the curve in time to see Susan's car in the lead pull as close as she could to the bank. She wrestled the case out the window and give it a push over the bank. I said a silent prayer that the Mercedes would keep driving. It did not. In the headlights of the redneck dream I could see the Mercedes pull in front and cut off her exit. "Trouble Olly, I shouted into the radio, get out now".

The driver of the tailing Mercedes calmly stepped out of his vehicle. It looked like an Uzi he carried but whatever it was it was big trouble. 3 things happened so quickly it seemed simultaneous.

As Susan tossed the case over the bank, the trunk of her car flew open and Olly bailed out armed with grizzly stopper ready for action. The lights of the 4x4 temporarily blinded the would be assassin, a second later the grizzly stopper roared hitting him square in the chest, knocking him backwards onto the hood of his own car, and the 4x4 hit the back quarter panel passengers side tail end of his car at good speed knocking it and the assassin over the cliff. The 4x4 barely slowed on impact, swerved back into the driving lane and sped off.

I bailed out with my loaded shotgun, Olly was doing the four direction hop looking down the barrel of his gun desperately searching for something else to kill.

The only thing in site was me so I started hollering "don't shoot me Oliver"

A second later, another black Mercedes came around the bend in an obvious rush. Fuck it, two quick rounds from my shotgun took out both headlights. The car had almost stopped when Olly opened fire. We both dived behind Susan's car as the muzzle flashes of and the quick chatter of an Uzi came from the back window of newly arrived car. I pumped another round into the chamber and fired where I thought had seen the muzzle flashes. Whoever these fuckers were, they were not nearly as tough when fire was being returned. We piled enough lead at them to discourage any plans they had for killing us. The firing stopped, the tires squealed, and they took off into the darkness with no headlights.

I used my last 2 shots to take out the taillights. Olly fired until his gun was empty then started to reload. "I think they are gone Olly, you can't hit them from here" as he fired one last newly chambered round in the direction they had went. "As long as there is lead in the air, there is danger boss" he replied, and then he ripped open Susans door exclaiming "Are you ok Susie?"

"I am fine" she said, I dived on the floor when all hell broke loose. What the hell went on, are you guys both OK?"

"We are fine as well but we need to get the fuck out of here now, get in my car, leave this piece of shit, it is bugged and full of holes anyway."

"Wait boss, I will go find the money" Fuck the money, lets get out of her alive"

"But Boss" he said before Susan cut in. "Leave the money Oliver, we will find it later."

Oliver stopped arguing as soon as Susan spoke. Jesus, I wished I could get Oliver to listen that well to me.

"Everyone into my car, I have another stashed for you guys. We will go get it. Same car as mine but different color."

Oliver escorted Susan to the car and opened the front passenger door. Always the gentlemen. WTF? I thought chivalry was dead but certainly didn't expect to see it revived in Oliver.

"Get in Oliver. There are some new toys for you and Susan in the back seat."

Olly ripped open a box and gave out some sort of a shriek and then started some strange cackling sound, seemingly to express his delight. Oh wow boss, just like Christmas only better" followed by more cackling with an intermittent sound that might be compared to a coyote with his balls caught in a bear trap.

"And look Suzie, one for you too" he squealed as he passed it to her in the front.

"Olly, stop fondling it and get them ready for action. I'm still trying to figure out who all wants to kill us, and why the fuck do they want to kill us so bad. Well, me and Susan confuses the shit out of me, but someone wanting you dead maybe not so much". Oliver was still stuck in his own little artillery heaven. Susan grabbed her shotgun out of Olly's hand, reached for the box of buckshot and started loading shells into the magazine.

Susan spoke. "I don't know who or why anybody wants to kill us but I am fucking over it. I am ready to shoot the first fucker I come to just out of spite. And I'd love to meet up with whoever the fucking chicken shits were that tried to off us on the way by in that last car." She pumped a round into the chamber. Bring it on motherfuckers, bring your fucking pop gun and lets get it on with this baby."

Jesus Christ sweet Susan. I created a monster. It must be Olivers influence.

Olliver interrupted my train of thought.

"Great night hey Boss? I think we each got to kill someone. Did you see grizzly stopper throw that fucker up on the hood of his car. Perfect timing. Right before the pickup accidently collided with his car and knocked them both over the cliff where they belong. And if there was a head behind that window you took out with the buck shot in the other car, it isn't attached to no neck anymore." He squealed with delight.

Note to self: I have to get some kind of humanity training for Oliver.

Right now, my priority objective was to get the fuck out of here before the Popo or more assholes who wanted us dead arrived or, the car that got away came back. It would be driving slow without headlights, and I didn't expect it to return but you never know. They were persistent bastards. I threw the malibu into gear and floored it intending to cut a hooker and blaze out of there. Didn't work. Fucking front wheel drives. The little car lurched ahead, and I had to hit the brakes, or we would have joined the Merecedes at the bottom of the cliff. I shifted to reverse and pinned the gas again. Worked better this time. It spun on the gravel and the front performed like it should making a 180-degree turn. I slammed it into drive, and it spun out on the gravel. The tires squeaked a bit when they contacted pavement, and the little shit box was up to 80mph in an amazingly short distance.

"Jeez Boss, settle down and slow down. Enough people trying to kill us without you doing the job for them" Oliver interjected.

He had a point. Chances were someone had heard gunfire and there may be some law enforcement enroute. A vehicle speeding from a suspected crime scene might seem suspicious. I said "Fuck off Olly" then slowed to the speed limit.

It was an uneventful trip back to the city and I relaxed a bit once we entered city limits where we could mix with the traffic and hide in plain site.

I drove aimlessly around the city watching closely for any vehicles that might be tailing us or anything suspicious looking. I even drove past Harcourt building to see what might be going on there but all was quiet. I circled the area I had left the spare rental car starting about 4 full blocks out, reversed direction a couple times. The adrenaline rush had subsided, and everyone was quiet, lost in their own thoughts until Oliver spoke up, breaking the reverie.

"What the fuck Boss? Where are you going? Are you lost? It is getting cold in here. Fuckers shot out our back window, there is couple holes in the door I am sitting beside and a bunch of shattered glass under my ass contributing to my discomfort."

That served to remind me. I was going to have to get myself another rental at the earliest convenience. In the daylight this one would tend to raise suspicion with the broken glass and random bullet holes here and there. And, I would have some serious explaining to do when I returned it to the rental company.

"Relax Oliver, I will have your ass off the glass and into a vehicle with windows and no bullet holes in a couple of minutes."

Susan chuckled, "Gotta take good care of the big ass. Your big ass has saved my ass more than once recently."

Susan's comment had lightened the mood and reminded me that Oliver had taken a load of buckshot in his ass preventing it from reaching my ass on a previous case.

Absolutely Oliver, your ass has become a very valuable asset, excuse the pun, in terms of blocking shotgun pellets and other possible gun fire from reaching it intended destination which was my ass on at least one occasion." I chuckled.

"Ok, OK," Oliver said, "disregarding the welfare of my ass, where do we go from here? There is at least a couple of bad guys who got away. I am pretty sure tonight's group was just henchmen, and word will have gotten back to the brains of the operation, whoever the hell that may be that we are still out here undeterred and not smart enough to quit. To save all of our asses it may be necessary put some more bad asses to sleep permanently." He chuckled although I didn't see a lot of humour in that.

"I have a plan Oliver" I said which was mostly bullshit. I had a plan to keep us alive in the short term but a long-term solution continued to evade me. I had some suspicions but still did not have a clear vision of the who was behind it all. The "what" was clear enough. Money was behind it. If the who was the Jackals, we had successfully incurred the wrath of a very dangerous and large criminal organization.

"That's why you are the boss, Boss, would you be so kind as to enlighten us on what this plan may be?"

"Of course, Oliver. Our immediate need is to find a safe place to get some R&R and for you to attend to your ass issue. Maybe put a little cream on it. Some antibiotic ointment is good." I said as I pulled up to the spare rental.

I passed him the keys to the car, reached into my own car glove box and pulled out an envelope with room door cards in it and passed those to Susan.

"These are for the Hilton downtown. Good security at the door. Once into your rooms you should be ok. They are adjoining rooms so keep the door open between them, and Oliver, you sleep with your grizzly stopper and maybe the shotgun as well if you don't mind a threesome. Susan you keep your shotgun close by as well. There is a duffle bag with some necessities in it, toothbrush, wigs, makeup etc., but plenty of room for the shotguns in the car. You can put the weapons in it to get them up to your room. No one should know that you are there. The rooms are reserved under a corporate entity called Giggles.com. I took the liberty of checking in and getting the door fobs, so you won't have to check in at the desk. Oliver the wigs and makeup are for disguise not for you to get in touch with your feminine side. Any questions?

"What about you Boss, are you coming with us? Oliver asked.

"No Oliver. Our main concern is getting a safe place for Susan where she can get some rest. I will be plying my investigative skills incognito. I am expecting a major shit storm to start and expect the storm will start at McCurdy investigations office complex." I grinned trying to keep the mood light. Oliver chuckled' "good one boss, we can use that as a code word, meet you back at the complex instead of see you at shits and giggles hole above the Chinese restaurant"

"Not a bad idea Oliver, never know when someone is listening so henceforth, the 3 of us shall refer to it as the complex, agreed?

Both gave me the thumbs up.

Oliver added, "But Boss, I still don't think you should be at your office by yourself. You have made a lot of enemies with some pretty bad people recently. Your natural charm and charisma have not been working that well for you as of late."

"No worries Olly, I am a big boy now, and I will keep my radio turned on and charged, to communicate with you. If I get in a spot I can't handle or If I am entering a high-risk situation, I'll keep the transmit button pushed so you can monitor the situation. Just don't verbally respond to me over the airwaves."

"Ok boss, but when this is over, I promise to give you a few pointers on exuding charm and resolving conflict".

Susan chuckled at that and said, "now boys, settle down, we don't have time to get into a battle of wits. And I could use a shower and some sleep."

"Ok, Lets get you moved into your vehicle and out of here." I opened the car consul.

"Here, help yourself to some extra ammo."

They each grabbed a handful and exited my car.

I waited until they had all their gear transferred to their vehicle and waved as they exited the lot.

I would have to abandon this rental where it sat but didn't think it was a good idea to walking around with my shotgun and other gear, so I put the 38 in my pocket and moved the rest into the trunk, locked the vehicle and took the keys. The broken back window would invite any nefarious thieves to investigate but with nothing inside to steal, hopefully the thieves would be discouraged and move on. I would have to return and get my toys after I had another rental.

I started the six-block trek back to my "complex."

When I was within a block from the rear stair entrance, I could see the flashing red lights of the emergency vehicles in the restaurant parking lot. Shit, that can't be good, I thought and considered reversing and just getting the hell out of there but my curiosity got the better of me. I had some of my disguise materials in a bag with me, considered donning something, reconsidered thinking what the hell. They are not going to shoot me in front of the ERT people and probably police attending as well.

I continued my path nonchalantly. Just a guy returning home from a late-night walkabout.

As I got closer, I could see the response team attending to someone on the ground, back doors of the ambulance open. They were about to place the casualty on a stretcher. The casualty appeared to be unconscious. Next to a squad car the police were questioning a man in handcuffs. They were standing with their back to me and turned as I approached. To no one's surprise sargent Morgan was attending the scene. To my surprise, it was my friendly rum souse in handcuffs. The seemingly alleged perpetrator's eyes widened when he saw it was me.

"You, you, you fucker. You the fucker who steals my whiskey," he shouted. He turned and addressed Sargent Morgan. "Its him, he is the guy. The fucker assaults me and steals my whiskey when I come here." He was trying to point at me with his nose seeing as his hands were cuffed behind his back. I whispered, "it was rum, dumbass."

Morgan ignored him and turned to me. "Well, well, if it isn't shits and giggles chief executive officer. Imagine finding you at the scene of a crime. Wonders never cease.

"I am sorry officer; I do not understand. I have been out for a late-night stroll am just returning now. Has there been a crime committed? Has my office been breached? I have a lot of valuable and confidential information in there."

"Him, him," the drunk said' he's the fucker you should arrest and put in jail. Whiskey thief and assaulting bastard."

Morgan turned to him briefly. "Shut the fuck up," he said.

Morgan leaned against his car then addressing me he said, "According to this gentleman, he nodded towards the cuffed guy, he has been repeatedly assaulted by someone at this location. Somone apparently assaults him, steals his whiskey, and leaves him for dead every time he comes around here. "Jeez, that's terrible sir, I don't know what the world is coming to. Perhaps you should advise him to not come around here." I suggested. We were interrupted by and extremely agitated Chinese lady poking me in the chest. "you, all a time is trouble whit you since you rent here. I tell to my husband he should evicts you."

Morgan giggled a bit. I did not know he was capable of that.

"Christ McCurdy, you seem to have all your neighbors mad at you. Pretty soon I will be the only friend you have left." More giggles.

"As always Sargent, I appreciate your undying friendship and your absolute dedication to the good of the community" I replied.

"Yeah, yeah, cut the bullshit McCurdy, what have you got yourself into that requires late night strolls to calm your nerves, and where the hell are you strolling from? I notice a shiny new Mercedes sitting out front. Would that not be more comfortable for you? "That is not mine sir, it is a temporary loaner from a client, and I would not damage her trust in me by overusing it when I am perfectly capable of walking. As you mention, it is a genuinely nice vehicle."

Morgan pushed himself upright off the car, "Um hm, that it is. Much to classy to belong to shits and giggles incorporated. I took the liberty of running the plate and it is registered to Harcourt holdings limited. I am beginning to question the safety rating of these vehicles. Just recently one was found at the bottom of a cliff just outside the city and as soon as I leave here, I have to attend another incident involving a similar vehicle over the same cliff also registered to Harcourt holdings. Is it possible that Harcourt Holdings is your client?'

With all due respect sir, I am not at liberty to discuss my client. Client investigator confidentiality issues. I am sure you understand," I replied.

"Yeah, no shit. What I understand McCurdy is that you are an uncooperative dumbass and you have gotten in to shit that may be well over your head. The victim they are loading on the stretcher over there does not have any identification on him. I do not suppose you have met him before or have any inclination as to why he may have been trying to, possibly illegally judging by the tools he carried, access your business premises this time of night?

"No, to the first question, and none whatsoever to the second question." I said. Perhaps I owe this gentleman a debt of gratitude for preventing that." I nodded at the guy in cuffs.

"Yeah, I am sure he is just a good Samaritan jus being mindful of his community," Morgan turned to the ERT activity. "It appears our victim may be waking up. You stay here. I am going to see if I can ask him a couple questions. And don't assault our good Samaritan while I am away."

The drunk put his head own and peered up at me suspiciously. "You heard what he said, stay away from me. I would kick your ass except for these cuffs holding me back."

"Buddy," I said, when this is over, I am going to buy you the biggest bottle of rum you ever seen for stopping that intruder. Maybe we can discuss an employment position as security guard.

He grinned, "make it rum dumbass."

Morgan came swaggering back over. "Well, all the gentlemen seems to be able to remember is he was here to pick up the Mercedes. Says you were supposed to return it.

Strangely enough he can remember that but cannot seem to remember his own name, where he is from or anything else. Middle eastern looking fellow. His accent would tend to confirm that as his origin."

"Welcome to America where neighbors are friends and look out for each other." I said.

The drunk nodded his agreement, "Yep, that's what we do." he said.

"Well," Morgan said, "I would love to stay and chat but duty calls. I have to get on out to that other incident. Appears there are some fatalities that may have been deceased before the Mercedes took the dive. I may be judging Mercedes steering and braking capabilities prematurely. The patrolman at the scene says a body in close proximity to the vehicle has a large hole in his chest. You would not have any insight into that would you McCurdy?"

"None whatsoever" I said. "BTW sir, if you could uncuff this gentleman and free him up on his own recognizant, he will be gainfully employed as my security guard for the evening."

"Ah, what the fuck," he said as he removed the handcuffs. He reached in the car, pulled out the bat, and passed it to the drunk. "Security guard in this neighborhood needs to be armed" he grinned.

As Morgan drove away the drunk turned to me holding the bat like he was waiting for a first pitch. "My rum?? he questioned.

I took a 100 dollar bill out of my pocket and passed it to him.

"Wages," I said, "take the rest of the night off" and I headed up the stairs to my office.

"Much appreciated," he said, then added, "Boss."

Sometimes I do stupid things. Lately I have done a lot of stupid things.

I climbed the stairs to my office, tried to enter as quietly as possible. I did not know for sure if the place was bugged but the potential was there so hopefully no one would know I was inside.

Number one priority on my list was sleep. I put my phone on mute, texted Oliver to ensure they had arrived safe and sound in the rooms. All was good so I secured the doors, set some chairs and other obstacles behind the doors that would make some noise to wake me up should someone breach the door, loaded my revolver and put it under my pillow, turned phone on to vibrate and placed it and the two-way radio on nightstand. In seconds I was sleeping soundly.

I was sleeping soundly when my phone buzzed indicating I was getting a text. The clock said 7am.

My first thought was that I needed a shot of rum. A hair of the dog that bit me to clear the cobwebs until I remembered I hadn't had time for a drink since I met the lovely Susan Harcourt. Felt like a hangover but alcohol could not be the problem. I settled on blaming it on coming down from the adrenaline rush of being shot at lots.

I shook out the cobwebs and rolled off the bed. I was still fully clothed. The text was from Oliver . *Just checking to make sure everything ok boss, Everything is cool here.*

I texted back. *All is good. Stay where you are. Order room service if you need anything but stay where you are until I contact you again,* I replied. The phone buzzed again. I glanced at the screen to see a thumbs up emoji indicating Olly had received and agreed.

CHAPTER 13

First thing I needed was some transportation.

My brain had what I thought at the moment was a brilliant idea. There were lots of vehicle rental places at the airport. It would involve some risk but I was thinking if I take the bugged Mercede to the airport and leave it in long term parking, get inside and rent another vehicle, the bad guys may think we had all jumped a plane and left town. The risk was that as soon as it moved there was a good possibility there would be a gang of thugs looking for it. Good possibility there was someone watching the car and my office right now. I peered out my window at the street below. No black Mercedes in sight but that meant nothing. I could not see any vehicles sitting with occupants in them.

One hippy van with blacked out windows in the parking lot across the street and down about a block.

My mind shifted to the prior evening's events. The accidental victim who absorbed the clubbing intended for me had the appearance of a middle eastern heritage and Sargent morgan seemed to confirm that from his accent. My only observation was that he was well dressed, a dark suit, and his complexion was dark skinned, but he was not African American. Could have been Mexican, aboriginal American, Inuit, or a host of other ethnic groups. I had been around long enough to know that the majority of people were good and decent regardless of the heritage but also there were some downright snakes in the grass rotten bastards among them all.

My prejudices were against snake in the grass rotten bastards. Everyone else I considered to be friends I hadn't met yet. I was pretty certain I was going to meet some snake in the grass rotten bastards before the day was over, but WTF. May as well get the party started.

I texted my intent to Oliver, put the revolver in my jacket pocket, grabbed the Mercedes keys and headed down the backstairs. I would make my way to the street in front, get in the Mercedes, and bolt for the airport.

As I exited the building, I found my newly hired security guard, sort of at his post, on the ground reclining against the building, bat in one hand, bottle in the other, fast asleep.

I questioned his work ethic in my mind but then remembered I'd given him the night off so technically speaking, he was not on duty, and seeing as I am not the morality police, it was none of my business what he done in his free time.

Frankly, I was surprised to see him at all. I never expected to see him again but perhaps that was just wishful thinking.

I made my way down the sidewalk between buildings to the street where the Mercedes was parked. My spider senses were on high alert, watching for anything suspicious. Whoever the rotten bastards that were intent on killing us were, they had proven they were not above a sneak ambush.

As I rounded the front of the building, I was ambushed but not by any nefarious rotten bastards. The building owners, wife and husband intercepted me with demands to pay my rent. My cash supply was running low but I had enough to pay them and I did. Another stern lecture from the lady who insisted to her husband that I was always just "trouble, every time is him he just cause a trouble" just kick him out of building, yes I think and no more trouble."

Fortunately, the husband didn't think I was all that much trouble. He said something in Chinese to her and shook the handful of cash at her. I left them to their argument and jumped in the Mercedes and fired it up.

One thing about the Merecedes brand, it was not short on power. The ride and handling were pretty good as well. I was travelling well over the speed limit as I approached the off ramp leading to the airport. I had been on the lookout for any suspicious vehicles or some one tailing me. My keen sense of observation somehow missed the speed trap the local law enforcement had set up. I hit the brakes much too late, noted by my keen sense of observation as I watched as the speedometer pass below the 100 mph mark.

Fuck sakes, just what I need I said to myself aloud. While my mind considered taking evasive action, the trooper turned on the flashing blue, red, and white lights to indicate I was to make an immediate stop, executed a perfectly performed police turn, and fell in behind me. I had a good lead but no place to run. Options were taking the exit into the airport where I would surely meet an abundance of airport security as well as police, or continue straight on the interstate, pull an OJ Simpson, and give all the television channel something interesting to air on the evening news.

I continued braking and took the exit to the airport, pulling to the shoulder lane, slowing to a crawl, removing the revolver from my jacket and stuffing it under the bench seat of the Mercedes as I searched for a safe place to stop. I followed the ramp curve to the bottom where it leveled out, pulled well to the right of the parking lane, and stopped. I noted airport security flashing lights headed my way as well. "Fuck" I cursed under my breath, bad time to be creating a scene. WTF? Seemed like a lot of attention for a speeder.

The trooper pulled in behind me and stopped, lights flashing. In my rear-view mirror, I watched the driver's door open, a trooper steps out and aims his revolver over the open door. The passenger's side door opened, and a second trooper stepped out behind his door aiming a shotgun, not unlike my own, in my direction.

"Put your hands in the air and step out of the vehicle" he shouted.

With that much firepower aimed my direction I was more than happy to comply. I pushed the door open and reached out, both arms raised and hands in open position, waving so they were sure to see both hands empty. "Walk backwards toward me" the trooper shouted. I done as instructed as an airport security truck pulled in front of the Mercedes blocking any plans of an exit should I be stupid enough to try that. I was not that stupid.

The passenger side trooper kept his shotgun trained on my back while the driver side trooper approached me from behind. "Lay face down on the ground" he instructed. I done as instructed. The trooper placed his knee on my back, much more forceful than was necessary, placed one cuff on my raised right hand, pulled it over to meet the left hand and clamped on the handcuffs. Much tighter than was necessary. He removed his knee from my back and lifted me to a standing position using my arms for leverage causing me to wince at the pain transferred to my shoulder rotator cusps.

He pushed me onto the trunk of the Mercedes face first and started the standard procedure pat down. In an effort to gain some comfort level, I turned my head so to the right and laid my cheek on the trunk. From that vantage point I could watch the curiosity seekers slowly driving past on their merry way to the airport to pick up loved ones, business colleagues, or headed off to unknown destinations. Strangely enough, I thought I recognized one vehicle. The hippy van with the blacked-out windows that had been parked near my office this morning. Perhaps being in the custody of law enforcement at this moment in time was a good thing. I still did not appreciate it. Feeling confident that I would not be shot by either the good guys or the bad guys, I felt comfortable enough to start exercising my indignation at being so cruelly treated by law enforcement. "What the fuck? So. I was speeding a little bit. Give me a ticket and fuck off. I need to call my lawyer right now please." When no one responded, I emphasized the point. "As in right fucking now, please. I know my rights. I tried to ensure the indignation was evident in my voice."

"Actually, the trooper said, you were going a whole bunch to fast. But that is the least of your worries." He leaned towards me and raised his voice to emphasize his point of view. "You were going way to fucking fast in a fucking stolen car that was reported to have been stolen by drug traffickers." He calmed. "The canine unit is on the way and will confirm the contents of your stolen vehicle. Buddy, you fucked up royally when you heisted this vehicle."

I could not think of anything productive to add to the conversation so stood with my mouth open, Duh look on my face. My brain needed a minute to process that information. Stolen!! WTF was up with that? And stolen full of drugs?? I would have to talk to Oliver and Susan, however the nice trooper removed my phone from my jacket and was busy scrolling through my personal text messages at this moment. Good thing we all had burner phones. Contact for Oliver was "A" and contact for Susan was "B". I could hear it vibrating in his hand from incoming notifications.

"Excuse me officer, I said, if you could please stop going through my personal messages without a warrant to do so, and return my phone, I would sincerely appreciate it. I would like to contact my legal council".

He chuckled a bit, passed it towards me, then realized my hands were cuffed behind my back, and chuckled harder. "Yup he said, legal counsel A and legal counsel B seem to be frantically trying to reach you. They are probably wondering why your legal delivery is late." More chuckles.

The entire police force apparently were humorists. I had difficulty seeing any humor in my situation.

He turned me around and started to remove the handcuffs. There was no place to run to, but he felt the need to offer some advice. "If you think of causing any trouble, keep in mind that I would be nothing short of delighted to plant a couple of 9mm slugs in your back. Or front for that matter. Fucking dope dealing scum should all be dealt with on the side of the highway."

I rubbed my wrists to get some blood flowing.

"Thank you for the kind advice officer, and I agree, drug dealers should be shot and then pissed on at the side of the road, or at least the earliest convenience. Bad for tourism just leaving them to rot on the roadside.

However, fortunately I am not one of them. And the car is not mine, however it is a loner that I would be returning today if I were not pulled over on the side of the road being abused by agents of the law."

A police van pulled up and the driver, assumed handler of the canine unit, stepped out and opened the back door of the van. "Come on Charlie, time to go to work."

The dog, a mixed breed, probably a combination of Labrador retriever and German shepherd, maybe some collie mixed in, jumped out and went directly to the rear of the Mercedes, put his paws up on the trunk, stopped, looked over his back with his tail wagging, tongue hanging out of his mouth and panting. He looked up at me and I swear he was grinning.

I whispered "mutt" to him as though questioning his heritage may have some influence. It did not. He was staying put. The only thing to wait for now was to see what kind of Contraband Charlie the mutt had located.

The trooper who had made the stop came back from his patrol car after radioing in my ID. He passed me my wallet.

"So, you are a private dick, are you? He queried. "I prefer the term investigator. Dick is often used when describing a part of the male anatomy."

He walked past and up to the canine handler. "Let's wait to see what Charlie has found before we decide on the context it should be used in."

I had never considered myself a real fast talker so maybe today was an exception.

"Sir, I have never seen the inside of the trunk on that borrowed vehicle. Whatever is inside is not mine and you may want to consider getting permission from the owner or getting a warrant from a judge before searching it. Would not want to taint any evidence you may find.

"So now you are a fucking lawyer as well as a private investigator" he said, pronouncing investigator in a drawn-out fashion that made it sound more derogatory than dick. "I believe I know what context to use the word dick in. I think you are just a plain old dickhead, screw the private part.

"Just saying" I said, motioning with open hands gesturing submissiveness.

While trooper a was considering this new concept of human rights, tires squealed a bit on the pavement as a another cruiser skidded to a stop.

It did not surprise me in the least to see that Sargent Morgan was the new arrival. And frankly, for the first time in the history of our relationship, I was not disappointed to see him.

"What the hell is going on now McCurdy? Every time the radio goes off in the precinct with a call of some kind of goat fuck issue to attend to, I arrive to find Shits and Giggles Investigations at the heart of it. By the way, where is giggles. He wasn't with you last night and I haven't seen him around for awhile. Seems that his unique brand of charm and charisma may be beneficial in keeping your sorry ass alive."

He looked at the dog still standing with front paws up on the Mercedes trunk. "What's in the trunk?" he asked, not directing the question to anyone in particular.

Trooper A said, "we have not opened it yet sir. The private investigators suggest there may be some issue with warrants or permissions that would spoil any evidence.

"Fuck what the Gumshoe has to say, open the trunk." trooper B had a crowbar ready for any opportunity to use it. And as he raised it, I said "Wait, the gumshoe would like to suggest you push the little button just to left of the steering wheel under the dash. Keys are in the vehicle, and it should open the trunk."

Disappointed looks all around that there would be no requirement for destruction of the Mercedes. Trooper B moved to the driver's door, located the release button pushed it and opened the trunk.

"Just like magic," I said. Morgan said, "Oh fuck off" and moved to look in the trunk. He pulled out a small duffle bag, opened it and examined the contents.

"I got to say McCurdy, I'm not impressed. Maybe a kilo of pot, some baggies with white powder, probably cocaine, but no body or even parts of a body. These past few days, every time I have seen one of these fancy Mercedes cars there has been some blood and gore and other signs of mayhem in close proximity to them. All the vehicles registered to Harcourt holdings, flying off cliffs, full of bullet holes, makes me think there might be more to it than just offshore manufacturing quality control issues. I do not suppose you would have any thoughts or opinions on that, would you Mr. private investigator."

"Gumshoe is fine sir. And, as you know the scene you attended to last evening in which my security guard intercepted an alleged break in, into my office, the perpetrator of that alleged break-in claimed he was only there to retrieve a vehicle, which he maintained was stolen and which I maintain is a loaner. This would be that same vehicle sir and I was merely attempting to get into the rightful owner's possession. I confess that I was exceeding the speed limit slightly and as such I deserve to be ticketed, so if you could have your friends here write me up for that, I would suggest we put and end to this experience and get out of here so traffic can move freely and onlookers can get on with their day. All these vehicles and flashing lights are creating a traffic hazard.

And, I too have serious concerns of with non north American manufacturers quality control which is why I personally will only own north American made vehicles."

Morgan ignored me. "Ok people, he said, Party is over, I can take it from here. Get this piece of shit vehicle towed to the crime lab for further investigation."

My phone continued to vibrate in my pocket from Olly and Susan trying to reach me. I took the opportunity to send a quick text to alleviate their concerns. *All good. Will contact shortly.*

Trooper A looked a bit disgruntled at being overruled by a higher rank but proceeded to bark orders clearing the scene.

Captain Morgan turned his attention back to me.

"Get in my car McCurdy, we need to talk."

I knew I was about to get a lecture / interrogation but felt more comfortable with Morgan than a bunch of trigger-happy rookies. I got into the passenger's seat trusting that Morgan was ok with that. Never was fond of back seats in police cruisers. No door handles.

Sargent Morgan got in the driver's seat. No mention of me not in back seat. That was a good sign.

He sighed and rubbed his chin.

"McCurdy" he said, "I do not know what the hell is going on. The only thing I know for sure is that you are full of shit when you try to tell me you do not know anything about what is going on."

I thought it was best to just keep my mouth shut. I could think of nothing to say that would not be seen as total bullshit because that is what it would be.

Morgan shifted and leaned on his door getting comfortable.

"Just between you and me my friend, I would avoid any black Mercedes. This is the third one I have encountered recently. The first two had obvious signs of death associated with them, and some obvious evidence of homicides with regards to at least one. I kind of expected to find your body in the trunk this morning but, perhaps that was just wishful thinking." Bit of a chuckle at his own humor.

He continued, "Now, I have known you for a long time and I know you are capable of some actions that are lower than a snake's tit in a wagon rut, however I don't see the drug trade as being your forte. I don't think you are smart enough for that industry. (bit of chuckle- good to see his sarcasm was in good working order)

If I had searched that vehicle last night, I may or may not have found the measly drug stash in the trunk, however I do not believe you had anything to do with putting it there." He paused then continued, "Now, all of these shiny vehicles involved in the various mayhem are registered to Harcourt holdings limited. My deductive powers suggest that would be just a bit much to consider coincidence. Would your superior deductive powers agree with mine?"

I ignored the obvious sarcasm in the question. "Yes sir, that does sound like a bit much," I agreed.

"SOOO, Morgan continued, seeing as both great powers of deduction agree, I took the liberty of doing a bit of checking on this Harcourt Holdings limited," he emphasized the limited, "to see if I could ascertain a possible reason for these coincidences."

I waited for more info.

He started again. "At first glance they seem pretty legitimate and clean. However, one of the fingerprints lifted out of one of the vehicles belongs to a Mohammad something or other who is currently on USA' no fly list for suspected terrorism." He stopped to let than sink in. I admit it was a bit unnerving for me. Morgan waited for my reaction.

"Hmm, I said, sounds like that guy should be shot and pissed on."

Morgan shuffled back into the driver's seat.

"Yeah, thing is, I am thinking he or they may want the same for you. Is it possible they may have already tried unsuccessfully to accomplish that. It would appear you have gotten yourself on the wrong side of some very nasty people, McCurdy."

He paused but I said nothing. Might as well let him vent for awhile.

"Of course, if someone wants to kill you, that is none of my business, in fact I cud empathize wit them.

However, I worry the tactics they may employ killing you, may cause some collateral damage that could injure some honest citizens in my town. Citizens that I have sworn to protect, and that concerns me greatly. Let me explain. It pisses me off to no end. Issues me off more than shits and giggles everyday run of the mill aggravates the beejeezuz out of me.

"I understand and appreciate your concern sir" I said.

The Canine handler interrupted with a knock-on Morgan's window. He was holding my revolver between two gloved fingers. Morgan rolled down his window. "This was located under the front driver's seat sir" the trooper said. Morgan stuck a pen in the barrel to retrieve the weapon. "Thank you", he said to the trooper and then turned to me still with the revolver on the end of his pen. "If I take this to forensics, is it possible I would find your fingerprints on it?" He asked.

"Yes sir, there is a distinct possibility of that outcome. I am licensed to carry a concealed firearm." I reached for my wallet to produce the licence. Morgan waved his hand, "Yeah, yeah, I believe you. This state they give anybody a licence to carry. You, McCurdy, are a walking advertisement for gun control. And your partner Oliver is as bad or worse. For Christ sakes had a report from a lady in his apartment building that he was trying to shoot her cat. I think he may have some mental issues."

"I agree Olly may have some mental issues and, now that you mention it sir, regards myself, you may be echoing my mother, rest her soul, who suggested I was a walking advertisement for birth control when I was a child. Perhaps it is my natural evolution of my career cycle?"

We both had a bit of a chuckle with that.

"Ha, ha, your mother was a wise woman McCurdy, too bad you missed out on some of that in your genes. He chuckled for a minute, at his own wit, then went on, "So anyway, if you would care to share any information with me on what the hell you are involved in, I may be able to help keep you alive or at least minimize the mayhem revolving around you."

"Thank you, sir, and all jokes aside, I do mean that sincerely. It is just that, well, you know how it is with client confidentiality."

Morgan shifted back to the driving position with a groan.

"Yeah, yeah, we will put that on your tombstone. Here lies a confidential son-of-a-bitch. And, seeing as dead people don't talk, perhaps, if you could leave me a note in your will with any information you may have on who killed you, it would save me some groundwork."

"Will do as advised sir," I replied.

"Ok, where in hell do you want to go? That car is being towed so I would be happy to drive you wherever you would like to go. Preferably another state where you may consider permanent residency the hell out of my city."

"Much appreciated sir, but if you would be so kind as to drop me at the airport to which I was enroute would be great, thank you."

I added, "You know, captain, we are on the same team. Law and order, catching bad guys, etc. We could be friends."

"Yeah, we could be friends McCurdy, if only you were not such an asshole."

Morgan stopped the car in front of the departure gate.

"See what that sign says McCurdy, Departures. Take my advice and get on a plane going anywhere and depart. And don't come back. Maybe you can stay alive, and I can get some peace. You may need this." He passed me back my gun.

"Thank you for the advice, sir," I said as I stepped out of the car.

All things considered that had gone rather well. The fact that Morgan had showed up and overruled the rank-and-file law enforcement had gotten me out of jam, however I was now back at risk from the assholes who wanted me, Susan, and Oliver dead. I Assumed Oliver and Susan were safely holed up in the hotel. I dialed Oliver on the burner phone as I walked the length of the airport looking for a vehicle rental.

"Boss, are you ok, what the hell is going on?" Oliver shouted into the phone before it finished the first ring.

"I am fine Oliver, I just got a speeding ticket, I will explain later," I downplayed the goat fuck situation I had been in.

"I am at the airport picking up a different rental vehicle. One without so many bullet holes in it. Order me room service breakfast and I will join you in an hour, give or take," remembering I had to go back to the other rental and pick up the weaponry and ammunition I had stashed in the trunk.

"How are you guys doing? Anything suspicious going on?

"No, all is good here boss, we haven't left the room, just ordered room service a couple times. All rested, fed, happy and ready to come out to play anytime. We will see you when you get here." He ended the call.

I requested a pickup at the rental counter and got a 4x4 extended cab unit with no markings on it. Something a little more durable. It would not stop bullets but more capable of travelling rough terrain should the circumstances dictate the necessity of some evasive maneuvers.

First stop after leaving the airport with my new rental, was my old bullet riddled rental car to retrieve the weaponry stashed in the trunk. Having done that I considered a quick check in at my office, decided it was relatively low risk, so made the short walk. Finding my newly appointed security guard at his post, trusty bat in hand sitting on the steps. I passed him a couple hundred bucks to replenish his supplies and requested a report on any suspicious activity.

"couple guys sitting in a vehicle out front and every now and again they make a lap through the parking lot in the back here but no one has tried to get inside," he tapped his bat on the steps and grinned.

"Good job man," I said, as I moved past him and up the stairs to my office. In the office, nothing seemed out of the ordinary, so I quickly found an empty grocery bag, stuffed my blond wig and other disguise materials in it, and headed back to get my rental truck. Once the vehicle was moving, I donned the blond wig, a pair of clear Roy Orbison type glasses, and placed a floppy cowboy hat on top of it all. I made several loops around the downtown core area watching for any tail I may have picked up. Comfortable that I was not being followed I went to the hotel to join Oliver and Susan.

My old long haired hippy cowboy disguise I received some slightly strange looks from security and the front desk clerk, but no one interrupted me as I got on the elevator and pushed the button for the fifth floor. On the third floor a couple of over made-up ladies who had obviously had an early start on the champagne got on. I politely ignored the flirtatious "hey cowboy" comment with a smile. My paranoia was getting the best of me. I exited alone on the fifth floor and proceeded to Oliver's room.

I knocked on the door. After a moment in which I was sure Oliver was peeking though the little spy glass, the door opened, and the grizzly stopper was pointed in my face. "Is that you boss?" Oliver queried, squinting quizzically at my cowboy get up. "Yes, it's me Oliver, let me in." He stepped back from the door, and I entered to a couple of strange sights. One, Oliver was standing there in his boxer shorts, 250 pounds of Shrek meat, and two, Susan was sitting on the bed in pajamas with the 12 gauge pointed my way. "Oh, sexy cowboy, she smiled"

Olly closed the door, "Good to see you boss, you had us worried about you. You have to let us know when you going to be dressed up all weird. I was thinking about shooting you right through the peep hole. Probably would have except I kind of recognized the wig I tried to drown."

"Point taken Oliver, where is my breakfast?" I asked looking around at the empty trays.

"Sorry boss, it was getting cold, so I ate it." Susan spoke for the first time. "I will get one delivered right away" she said picking up the house phone.

I filled them in on my morning while waiting for my breakfast to arrive. I explained why I was leaning toward taking Morgan and the local law enforcement off the list of suspects considering Morgans behaviour and how he was actually my salvation from the goat fuck incident. The others were doing their job apprehending a car thief because it the vehicle had been anonymously reported stolen by drug dealers. That did not mean the bad guys were not getting information from someone in the law enforcement category but at least there was no evidence of a widespread conspiracy.

So, that left us with the jackals and Harcourt Holdings, perhaps a joint venture of the two. I had not seen the Bobbsey twins as of late, but I was inclined to believe they may be the Jackal connection. But WTF with the jackals? We were trying to do as they asked and drop off the cash, as instructed when all hell broke loose, and we had to vigorously defend ourselves from heavily armed assholes. Why would the Jackals want us dead for delivering the money they had demanded? Blackmailers tend to keep their victims alive so they can ask for more somewhere down the line. What point would there to be collect the ransom demand and then kill the source and the messengers,

Susan spoke of how little she was actually involved with the business side of Harcourt holdings but any time she has spent in the office building she noted there were quite a few people of middle eastern descent around. It was becoming obvious she did not know her husband all that well either. She had spent most of her time relaxing and being catered to in her new mansion courtesy of her husband. She mentioned that when she offered to become a productive support for her husband's business, he would put her off with how that was not necessary. She was unhappy with her situation because her life did not seem to have any purpose other than to sit in luxury and wait for her husband to come by occasionally. A trophy wife was not her life ambition. She reiterated what she had told me at our first meeting. That she had been swept off her feet and caught up in all the glamour and excitement and what she at first thought was opportunity but recently was starting to tire of being an object for Dustin Harcourt to show off. She felt she was just another piece of artwork like the Rembrandt Dustin had on his wall to show off to guests.

I personally was beginning to suspect she was an object to be insured and disposed of but didn't state as such out loud. The girl was a recent widow, still in mourning and now it was more than obvious she was a target. Someone wanted her dead very badly. It was me and Olivers job to protect her and that made us targets as well. Like Susan, that was beginning to piss me off big time. Jessica Baird was also on my radar screen. I could not get over how she provided a glowing reference for me without us having ever met. WTF was up with that. Way too many WTF's going on.

My business phone had been shut off for days, as I feared it could also be used as a tracking device. I set it on the counter and plugged it in to charge but would not turn it on until I was out and about and moving. I would make my way back to my office and turn it on to check messages then perhaps leave it there. Assuming we had successfully eluded our pursuers for the time being with untraceable communications it also eliminated any means of communication with the bad guys. Perhaps they had a change of heart and wished to surrender or call a truce and would be unable to let us know. Those were very unlikely scenarios I admit but was sure they had not forgotten about us.

I said as much to Oliver, and he just gave me a WTF is wrong with your head you dumb fuck look.

"OK, I said, I know that is stupid, but we can't just hide from them for the rest of our lives. We need a plan to lure them out, find out who they are and what their motives are."

"And then shoot all the fuckers" Olly interjected. Susan grinned and pumped her shotgun.

"Oliver, I would hope there was some other means, involve the FBI, Homeland security, the CIA, political leaders, the media, whatever, but I do not disagree, if those attempts fail, I am ok with killing all the bastards as well. I am not the morality police and sometimes bastards just need killing. It is the only way to stop them. Rid humanity of their existence."

"Ok, Boss, but while we are making all those efforts, if any bastards try anything, I am going to be shooting as many of the bastards as I can before FBI, CIA, or any of the rest of them show up."

There was no point in arguing with Olly. It was his natural survival instinct to simply remove any threats to his well being from existence. Or anything that bothered him really. A cat waking you up was not necessarily a threat to your existence but from Oliver's perspective, if it was dead, it would not be making any noise that may wake him up. An effective, albeit slightly unconventional system that worked well for him.

My breakfast had arrived, pancakes, sausage, bacon, hashbrowns, syrup, whipped cream, and fruit. Oliver's "instinct" reached for a slice of my bacon with one of his huge meaty paws and I whacked his knuckles with my fork. He had already had two complete helpings of breakfast. He said "Ouch, Boss, you could share."

"Fuck sharing, I am hungry" I said, and growled like a dog while taking a protective stance around my breakfast. Susan giggled. "Boys don't fight over your food. "She admonished like a mother hen. She was a hard one to figure out. Beautiful, bossy, motherly, threatening, and dangerous with a shotgun in her hands. More to her than the sweet, soft kitten I originally judged her to be. Add another WTF to my list of confusion.

I was way over full by the time my breakfast was done and had left one sausage behind. Oliver looked at the sausage, then at me to see if it was safe to reach for it. I nodded and he grabbed it and stuffed it in his mouth like a ravenous dog and growled a bit. I think he was trying to entertain Susan and it seemed to be working. She saw the humour in our bickering and sarcasm. She giggled again and she was even more gorgeous when she laughed or smiled.

I explained that my plan was to return to my office, turn my business phone on and check my messages. After last nights shoot out party, whoever the bad guys were, it had not gone well for them. My guesstimate was that besides property damage, they had probably suffered at least two fatalities. My instincts told me they were not the type of people who would take that well and would be looking for retribution vigorously. Not to mention they already seemed quite intent on making our whole trio dead from the get go.

I placed the blond wig back on my head and topped it with the cowboy hat, donned my Roy Orbison glasses and stood.

"I can swing by the mall on the way back if you guys need anything, just make me a list."

"I don't have a thing to wear boss, my chauffer suit is completely ruined, could you pick me up some pants and a shirt?

"I think I am ok for the day Susan" stated.

Ok just text me a list I said, then checked the bullets in my pistol, put it back in my jacket pocket, and stepped out the door.

I did not want to go anywhere near the bullet riddled rental so I cruised the area until I found a place, where I could park the pickup in the opposite direction from where I had abandoned the rental car. I found one less than two blocks away from my office entrance. I parked, checked my get up in the mirror, stepped out and headed down the back alley towards my office. About half a block from the restaurant parking lot I could hear a commotion going on. The Chinese lady restauranteur was in a very angry mood, and it wasn't me this time however it was unlikely my presence would improve her attitude. I moved closer to the hedge and made my way forward searching for a spot where I could observe without being seen. Probably better if I sit this one out and talk to my new rum guzzling

Melvin Deforest

security person after things calmed down a bit. Peeking under the hedge I could see another Mercedes, a bit older, kind of a shit brindle orange yellow color. The lady was armed with a formidable looking meat cleave chasing a dark-complexioned guy, definitely middle eastern dark, who was making a hasty retreat holding onto his right wrist with his left hand toward the vehicle.

"You go, you go now," she was screaming at him, all the while shaking the cleaver above her head in a very threatening manner. I had no doubt she would use it if she caught up to him. I think the guy running away was convinced likewise. "I go, I go, nice lady," he was saying in the charming mid east accent.

He made it to the vehicle, struggled to open the door with an obviously injured hand, but made it inside and slammed the door before the nice lady could do any blood letting. The nice lady was tapping the cleaver on his window and emphasizing he should go and stay away. He got the vehicle in gear and squealed the tires in reverse first, then struggled to get it into drive and squealed forward down the alley in the opposite direction from me. Having accomplished her objective, the nice lady walked back toward my security guy and for a moment I feared for his safety. It appeared, that she had sufficiently vented her frustration however and they stood, him with bat in hand, and her with cleaver lowered having a calm conversation.

I waited until she entered the building, stuffed the hat and wig inside my jacket, took the glasses off, put them in the left pocket opposite my pistol pocket, and approached the building.

"Boss" my man shouted as he noticed me approaching. "You missed all the excitement. That is one crazy little Chinese lady. She came to my assistance and put the run on that guy whom I had just stopped breaking and entering into your office quarters."

"Good job again man, I think you deserve a raise. Can you tell me what happened?"

"Sure, thing boss.

"I was on duty posted on the step when I see this vehicle pull up. Kind of a shit brown, yellow Mercedes. So, I step around the corner of the building out of site and he comes up to your door with that small pry bar laying over there" he pointed to the step. I glanced over to see what he was referring to. A small flat pry bar commonly used as a flooring tool.

"So, I jumps out with my bat, and I holler, hey, what the hell are you doing? He drops the bar and pulls a gun out of his pocket. I am not going to fall for that trick no more so I swing my bat at his wrist before he can get the gun pointed at me or hit me with it. He howled in pain and that is when the nice lady came to my assistance and put the fear of God into him shaking that cleaver and puts the run on him. He was on his knees trying to get hold of the gun again with his good hand, I think I may have broken the other hand, Fortunate for him he did not get hold of the gun because that pretty lady would have chopped his other hand clean off, I am sure. Did you see the size of that cleaver? Almost the size of a machete."

"I did not see it" I lied; however, I believe you, and I owe you both a debt of gratitude." I counted out five one-hundred-dollar bills and passed them to him. "Perhaps you could have lunch in her establishment and leave the lady a nice tip. I am afraid I am in a rush again so just have to run up to my office for a couple minutes and then get on to some urgent business that must be attend to. I unlocked the door and headed up the stairs. He called after me, "sure thing boss, thanks."

CHAPTER

14

I took my business phone out of my pocket, set it on the counter and plugged it in. It was at about 50% charge from the time it was plugged in at the hotel so would be good for the brief time I needed to check my messages. I was quite confident my security detail below would give me the privacy time I needed to check messages put took a quick peek out the front of the building. No Mercedes or other suspicious looking foreign vehicles however I did note the hippy van with the blacked-out windows was back where I had first noted it last time before I seen it again going past me at the airport. Fairly sure it was likely just a local vehicle and the passing at the airport was just a coincidence. I am not a big believer in coincidences.

With me security I place and ready to make a quick exit, I sat at my desk and turned on the phone. Ten texts and one voicemail. Seven texts were big prize winning opportunities where all I had to do was send my credit card information to receive enormous rewards, (scams) and two from Oliver when they were looking for me while I was being detained, and one recent said "Call this number if you wish to ensure the safety of Susan's parents, 555- 306-2225.

That was not good. I checked the voicemail.

I noted it was from the same number in the text. It was someone with a weird accent I could not define. "McCurdy, you have become a gigantic pain in the ass. I understand you are a total asshole, however that does not concern me. What concerns me greatly is that you are responsible for much property damage and severe injuries to some people in my employ. And now you have stolen our money. If you do not return this call within 2 hours there will be a delegation of mine flying to Kansas to attend to a certain farm site that Susan is very familiar with. On a personal note, my preference is to make executions quick and painless. Not so my delegation. Some of them have an inclination to enjoy torturing sweet helpless people." So far, the voice had been unreasonably calm. There was a slight pause and then he screamed into the phon. "Call me now you son-of-a-bitch."

This was not good. I checked the time of the text. It was over an hour and a half. I would have to call now.

I dialed the number. The same voice answered on the first ring.

"McCurdy, so good of you to call, and with time leftover, that is polite" he said in the same calm voice strange accent as most of the earlier call. I tried to keep the fear out of my voice and spoke. "Yeah, well I don't appreciate people calling my mother a bitch" I doubted we were ever going to be friends, so I was trying to sound tough. It did not seem to intimidate him in the least and did not improve his manners.

All calm again he said, "Ok you listen to me you motherfucker."

"Enough with the name calling" I interrupted him. "Cut the bullshit, What the fuck do you want?" I said, still being all tough. He still was not impressed.

After a short pause in which I could here him inhale, he went on. "You will meet us where we can discuss this situation uninterrupted in a place where we will not be disturbed. You will bring the lady Susan with you. You will bring the 2 million dollars you failed to deliver as promised last evening. The secluded beach where you had a previous encounter with one of my colleagues who was treated very unprofessionally by your thug is a good place. You may bring your thug if you choose, I leave that decision to you, however as you have been consistently unreliable in your dealings with us, I would suggest that he will be of little value to you. You will be waiting on the beach at seven pm. We can watch the sunset over the ocean. It is quite beautiful. If you are not at the appointed time and place. my private plane with the previously mentioned colleagues will be enroute to Kansas. I trust you understand and can comprehend the consequences of that. Goodbye." He disconnected the call.

Fuck, fuck fuck, not good. Very bad.

Ok McCurdy you gotta get your shit together and think. What to do? I was ninety-nine point nine-nine percent sure they were setting up an ambush. How could I make that backfire on them?

I left the phone on the counter, tucked my wig and hat back in my jacket, gun in pocket, and ran down the stairs. My security was absent from the steps which was a good thing. Probably having lunch with the nice crazy lady. I put the cowboy hat and glasses on as I was running to where I had left the pickup. I jumped in the truck and took a minute to put the wig under my hat, I peeled out of the alley and headed towards my sporting goods supplier. Probably a good idea to beef up my duck hunting supplies. On my way through the industrial area, I passed a metal fabrication / steel supply business. I had another brilliant thought so pulled in and purchased a 4x8 foot sheet of half inch plate steel and had them load it into the back of the pickup. Long box pickup so just the right size to lay flat in the box and still get the tailgate closed.

I stretched the speed limits on the way to the weapons supplier but did not break them. I did not want, or have time for, a repeat of this morning's event. I left the wig and glasses in the truck but kept the cowboy hat and walked looking down, so my face was partially hidden. I was not expecting to be spotted by the bad guys so just being extra careful. My paranoia gauge was starting to redline.

"McCurdy the duck hunter, how did that go for you?" the shopkeeper called as he saw me enter. "Not great" I said, "I can't get close enough to the buggers. Looking for something with a little more range today."

"Well, we can get you a lot more range with a hunting rifle," he said reaching for a rifle on the rack behind him. "This here is a 300 Winchester magnum. 4 power scope can get up to 12 powers for it, flat trajectory for 500 yards, noted for their accuracy. Bolt action with five shot clip. Packs a wallop. Duck, goose, moose, bear, or anything else does not stand a chance if they are on the receiving end of this baby." He chuckled.

"I'll take two of them, 6 clips, and 6 boxes of shells" I said. I did not have time to haggle or socialize.

He looked at me quizzically, obviously wondering what I was up to and then perhaps noticing I wasn't in the mood for socializing, said "As you wish sir, cash of course? "Cash it is, and please throw in a couple of gun cases for them, I will also take a set of that camo gear, pants and jacket largest size you have, keep the boxes the guns came in came in."

He rang the sale up, put them in gun cases as requested. I gave him cash and rounded it up to the nearest hundred as a tip, and no one seemed to take any notice of the cowboy walking out with two cased guns, a bag of ammo and camo gear. "McCurdy, your receipt he called after me." I never looked back.

At the hotel parking lot, I donned the wig, hat, and glasses. I left the newly acquired hunting hear in the truck.

No one paid any attention as I walked in the hotel lobby and proceeded to the elevator today. I was the only passenger on the elevator to the fifth floor. The door opened after a brief wait for Olly to check the spy glass. Oliver was still in boxers, so I threw the bag to him, and said, "for Christ sakes Olly, cover yourself up."

He grabbed the bag, opened it up, grunted an approval and went to the washroom to change. Susan had changed into jeans and boots that I had provided in the care package I left in the escape vehicle. She fit them very well.

I waited for Oliver's return before explaining the situation. I was genuinely concerned about how Susan would react to her family being threatened. I knew it would not be good.

Olly returned. "Looking pretty good hey boss, you done good, hat is a bit tight but ok" I hadn't realized the set came with a hat. It was stretched over the top of his head and emphasized the size of the size of his block head making him look a bit like a cartoon character.

I explained the details of my phone call and as expected Susan did not take it well.

No tears, just anger reflected in her face.

"As I see it guys, we have two choices. We can run, or we can confront them. Confronting them will be extremely risky," I said. "We can involve the Police, FBI homeland security, whoever and hope for some help."

Susan swung her legs off the bed.

"Nobody threatens my family. Those pricks think they can pull this shit, they are going to find out what cowgirls are made of."

"Susan, I was thinking that maybe Oliver and I could go it alone for this one. We could dress a mannequin to look like you to ride in the truck with me.

"I will be confronting them, with or without you" she stated putting and end to that discussion.

Oliver got out a "But Susan" before she shut him down. "No buts Oliver, I know I have put you guys in danger and I sincerely appreciate all you have done for me, but now it has gotten personal with these fuckers. I think I have been used and I do not like that. Threatening my family has crossed the red line. I agree with you that killing all the motherfuckers is a good plan."

"Ok then, it is decided. I will explain what I am thinking for a plan. There is a lot a stake for all of us so please help with any suggestions you may have."

The plan I had pulled out of my ass was not complex. If I was correct in thinking that they were setting an ambush, we would arrive early and ambush their ambush. Frankly, it scared the crap out of me. Past experience proved they were completely ruthless and had seemingly unlimited access to resources and firepower. The site they had chosen was the same site where they had previously ambushed us from the water and the sniper set up on the cliff overlooking beach where we had assembled. At her insistence, Susan would ride with me in the 4x4, and we would drive it onto the beach. We would take both vehicles. We would leave the car in the parking lot of the lounge and drop Oliver on the highway where he would find a perch overlooking the beach where he would be able to see us and to function as our sniper. Oliver would have the 300 Winchester magnum and most of the ammo for long range shots, plus the shotgun with buckshot and slugs for ammo and of course his trusty grizzly stopper for close quarters and short range. Buckshot was good for about 50 yards and the slugs were reasonably accurate to about 100 yards. We would be approximately 150 yards from Olivers nest. We would have shotguns with buckshot and slugs plus the one 300 Winchester magnum should we have the opportunity or necessity to use it.

If they employed the same two directional assault from land and water as before we would be more prepared this time. There was no guessing what they would have for firepower, automatic weaponry for sure, but suspected they may upgrade from the Uzi's to something with more range and kick like AK47's or similar. Susan and I would be on the beach out in the open. Essentially, we were the bait. I knew that Susan was their target, and I was just in the way so they may target me and then try to take Susan alive which was not going to be an easy task given her talents with a shotgun.

"OK, team, these assholes want to meet us. Are we ready? Radios are full charge, I checked. All weapons and ammo in duffle bag. Personally, I am scared shitless, how about you guys?" I said. "You got to have a brain to be afraid boss" was Oliver's only response.

"My anger is over-riding all of my other emotions right now Mr. McCurdy," Susan stated, I am just so fucking mad. Who do these fuckers think they are and what makes them think it ok for them to run around our country stealing, bullying. They need to learn that the strength of America and all democratic peace-loving nations is not dependent on the number of warheads or tanks you have. The strength comes from the heart of the common people who make up the nation. I am sure I will be shaking like a leaf for a few days when it is over. I will leave my scared shitless for a later occasion."

CHAPTER

14

5 o'clock pm.

We exit the room and down the elevator out of the hotel. Oliver tosses the duffle bag of weapons in the rental car. "We will meet you in the parking lot of the lounge at the beach Oliver, we will leave the car there as a backup and we will drop you back on the highway to find a perch in the bush on the cliff overlooking the beach. You can take the high-powered rifle and ammo then." Oliver just gave a thumb's up and got in the car.

Susan glanced in the box of the pickup and jumped in the passenger's side. Once we were in the truck and moving, she said. "What is with the plate iron in the box? Do you plan on building a tank?

"I am thinking they may have a sniper up on the hill where Oliver is going. That means they will be firing down on us, and the pickup walls are not thick enough to stop a high-powered rifle bullet. The 4x4 has lots of clearance so if they are firing at us from above, we can climb under the truck. That plate will stop just about any bullet. They are professionals so I expect a multi directional ambush. No place for them to hide along the coast, you can see for a mile at least in either direction so anything coming that route we should see them in time to prepare, maybe start our offense. A good offense beats a defense anytime. The ocean side, last time they came underwater and thanks to Oliver, it did not go well for them. We will have to keep our eyes out for anything suspicious approaching. Speedboats or even larger boats a distance out. If we are taking fire from that side, the only thing that will stop bullets on the pickup, are the engine block or wheel hubs. Take cover behind a front or back wheel."

"She said, "Sounds like you know a lot about this stuff, does it happen often?"

"Not really", I replied. "Some military training and enough hunting to know what a bullet is capable of," as we turned into the beach lounge parking lot.

Tensions were high and everyone was focusing on their inner thoughts, so conversation was limited. Similar to a military operation, the adrenaline was flowing, and each had their own way of dealing with it. Some people became aggressive, but most turned their thoughts inward when facing death. We were now the hunted. Unless you were a psychopath you did not enjoy killing, however nearly everyone was capable of it if it came to a kill or be killed situation. I was fairly sure that was the situation we were all walking into. Oliver stopped his car, and I pulled up beside him. He pulled the duffel bag out of the back seat of the car and climbed into the backseat of the truck. No words were spoken as I pulled out of the parking lot to go down the highway and drop Oliver where he could make his way into the woods and find a perch overlooking the beach. Oliver took one of the 300 Winchester magnums out of the case, worked the action, and then started loading clips. Oliver knew his way around firearms of all descriptions. "Nice boss" he commented.

I gave him one of the fully charged radios. He put it into one of the multitude of pockets on his camo hunting suit and started stuffing full clips and extra ammo in the other pockets. I also noticed he had a very large hunting knife to add to his weapon portfolio.

"We will maintain radio silence as much as possible but if you need backup Oliver, let us know and we will come with the pickup. He gave a thumbs up and stepped out of the truck. In a few seconds he had disappeared into the treeline.

6:10 pm.

We passed back through the lounge parking lot, past the boat launch, and past a sign that said "NO VEHICLES BEYOND THIS POINT, I asked "You ok Susan? She was a long way from her dental assistant career.

"I will be a lot more ok in a couple hours but yes, right now I am ok as I am going to be. My anger is till overriding all my emotions, and my common sense." she emphasized the common sense.

I kept the pickup as far up the beach close to the cliff drop off as was possible. When I thought we were approximately opposite Oliver's position, I turned the pickup to face the ocean, and backed in as tight as I could to the cliff. I checked my watch. It was 6:26 pm.

I The radio crackled. "Someone coming boss" Oliver whispered. I did not reply. Olly was on his own and hopefully he could handle the situation. Silence for about 4 minutes, then Oliver whispered. "All good boss, guy just dropped off a nice Kalashnikov for me. He has a very sore neck and won't be using the gun anytime soon", I could picture Oliver grinning. He had obviously taken out the land ambush portion of the deal. Or at least part of it.

I pressed the button to lower the window, and when I did, I could hear the drone of an airplane. About 500 yards out there was a small, twin engine aircraft following the coast at low altitude. Not necessarily bad news but my spider senses were on high alert. Just as I noted the plane to Susan, one wing dipped, and it made a sharp turn towards us.

"OH, fuck, fuck, I never saw that coming" I cursed and shouted at Susan. "Under the truck." As we both jumped out and rolled beneath the 4x4 box. "Oliver" I shouted into the radio, "attack from the air coming in from oceanside."

Just then I heard the crack of the 300 magnum. The plane dipped but continued its trajectory. We could now see the side of the plane with an open door and muzzle flashes from an automatic weapon strafing us. Susan lay prone under the box facing the incoming and firing her shotgun. The plane was still a bit distant for the buckshot to be effective but at least they new we were returning fire. At the same instant I heard the whoop, whoop of helicopter blades. We could not see the helicopter. He had approached from behind and was strafing the pickup. The sound of bullets hammering off the plate steel in the rear of the truck was deafening. More Fuck, fuck fuck I had not anticipated.

I could hear Oliver firing from up the hill to our left. It sounded as though he had upgraded to the donated Ak 47.

The helicopter was kicking up beach sand now as it hovered off to the right of the pickup attempting to get low enough to fire under the truck. Susan was reloading. As the landing skids of the helicopter came into view, I opened fire with my shotgun and buckshot. I was shooting blind from beneath the truck attempting to target an area above the skids. I did not know if I had caused any damage, but the chopper pilot appeared to have second thoughts and began to lift off in retreat. More automatic gunfire erupted from the hill off to our right. That confused the shit out of me. No way Oliver could have moved that far that fast. No idea who it was but they appeared to be targeting the helicopter and the plane. If they were firing on us, they had very bad aim.

After strafing our position the plane had circled over the water and was returning for another attempt. As the helicopter moved away I peaked my head out from beneath the truck. Susan was back in action and done the same.

"Target the stabilizer propeller on the back of the chopper," I shouted above the roar of gun fire and engine noise of the helicopter and the plane which was getting close again. As the plane was passing in front of us, I saw the pilot slump over the controls. Someone had made a hit. The now pilotless plane continued to arc back out over the ocean. I watched the stabilizer propeller on the helicopter disintegrate as Susan made a direct hit. The pilot was struggling to gain control and gain altitude when the now uncontrollable helicopters path intersected the arc of the pilotless plane. The plane and helicopter both disintegrated in a ball of flames.

The silence after the gunfire and air assault equipment noise had subsided, was both deafening and comforting.

Realizing it was over, Susan's lip quivered like she was about to cry.

I wanted to hug her but there would be time for that later.

"I know Girlie," I said, but right now we got to get the fuck out of here before the Popo arrives."

She tossed the shotgun in the box of the pickup and jumped in the passenger's seat as I climbed in the driver's side, praying this Ford would run long enough to get us out of here.

"Oliver," I shouted into the radio, "Are you ok?

"All good boss," you and Susie good?"

"We are good as well Oliver, and Susan will pick you up on the highway with the car. Get back to the hotel room and I will meet you there."

I was happy to see the Ford fire up and run. It was not until I started moving I realized that all of the tires were flat. I put the transmission in 4 high. With all wheels locked up I should be able to drive on flat tires until they came off the rims.

As we drove back to the lounge parking lot there was a group of people heading to the crash site. They were focused on getting to the crash site and paid little mind to a shot up ford with flat tires following the cliff bank.

I dropped Susan at the car and explained that I would head down the highway in the opposite direction from the city and get rid of the Ford so as not to draw to much attention. At the first off road I would abandon it and make my way back to the city. As I headed out the driveway of the parking lot, I was sure I caught a glimpse of the hippy van spin up some gravel as it turned out of the parking lot on to the highway towards the city. Another WTF? Too many coincidences in which I did not believe.

I hobbled the flat tired ford down the shoulder lane of the highway for about two miles and finally came to a campground. I turned in and searched for a convenient spot that would become the fords final resting place. There was steam rising from the radiator when I pulled it into the bush and shut it off. I would leave all the weapons with the vehicle and come back for them if possible. The one rifle had still not been fired.

I donned the cowboy hat and glasses, left the wig in the truck, and walked back to the highway to call a cab. I could hear sirens in the distance arriving at the beach.

The cab arrived with an extremely excited and talkative driver.

"Good evening, sir, where you be going?" "Just get me back into the city and I will decide from there, thank you." I needed some wheels but was pushing my luck with the rental company. I had rented three vehicles now under SAG (shits and giggles) Industries. Very creative name to my way of thinking. :) Two of them were now junk. I thought about borrowing from a friend but discarded that thought when it occurred to me that I didn't have any friends. The abandoned rental car was still driveable but was only in good condition if you compared it to the pickup truck. It still had air in the tires,

"Did you hear about the accident on the beach?" the driver queried. "No, I had not." I lied.

"Oh yes, is verry bad. Helicopter and airplane they collide in sky. Will be very bad. Everyone be dead. Cannot survive that, no, no. There be body parts floating everywhere. Nobody knows what happen. I think maybe they be drinking. At least one be drunk and run into other maybe. That is why I never be drinking and driving. Is verry dangerous. In fact, I never be drinking any ever. Is verry bad for you and verry dangerous for if you drive."

"I agree 100 percent my friend, just drop me at the hertz car rental downtown." I said trying to end the conversation. After some thought, I was thinking I could rent one under my own name. I did not think I had made any friends however the death toll for the bad guys had been very high the last few days. Hopefully the head of the snake was in one or the other of the crashed aircraft and as the driver had observed, no one can survive that. Maybe just my wishful thinking that there was nobody left to care about eradicating me or Susan.

The tv behind the counter of the rental place was on a news channel covering the accident scene. The on-scene reporter was saying the big question was who were they, and how did they manage to collide? More news at ten.

The who still confused the beejeezuz out of me. I had a pretty good idea on the how but would not be sharing that information.

The rental agency took no notice of me, and I left with a perfectly legal rental under the name of Melvin McCurdy.

My first stop was at a liquor outlet where I purchase to 66oz bottles of rum. My alcohol consumption had seriously declined lately, and I had some catching up to do. After that I swung by the back entrance to my office. My security guard and his trusty bat were at their post. I stopped beside him and powered down the passenger's window. "Jump in buddy," I said. His eyes lit up, "Hey boss," he replied as he climbed in. His eyes lit up even more when I passed him one bottle of the rum. "Where are we going? "I want you to meet a couple of my other friends. I do not think anyone will be around to bother my office today. I think you and I could both use a break and a shot of rum."

He smiled as he twisted the top off the 66er.

"It occurs to me that we have never been formally introduced to each other, I offered him my hand, "Melvin McCurdy, McCurdy Investigations."

He wiped his hand on his pants, "Joseph Johnathan Hamilton, retired from the marine core, you can call be JJ if you like." He said shaking my hand with a firm grip

Hmph, I thought, I never would have guessed that but did not verbalize my thought.

We arrived t the hotel and as I pulled into the parking lot I was struck with one more WTF? Jesus Christ, just for a day, I would like to go without a WTF. There sat the hippy van with the blacked-out windows. "Well", I said to Joseph Johnathan Hamilton, that is just too fucking much to be coincidence. That is a unique vehicle, and it keeps showing up everywhere I go. Usually when I see it there is a shit show of some kind going on where people are getting hurt."

"Oh yeah," JJ said, it is unique, and I kept seeing it around your office. It never stopped though and they never tried to break in. I was thinking it was just someone who lived close by."

I pulled my phone out of my pocket and dialed Oliver. He answered on the first ring. "Hi Boss"

"Is everything ok up there?"

"Everything is great up here boss, come on up."

I checked the bullets in my revolver and placed it back in my jacket pocket. The appearance of that van had my spider senses tingling.

Joseph Johnathan pulled his revolver out of his pocket. Still got his gun that B&E guy dropped when I whacked him with the bat.

"Good, just keep it hidden, bring the unopened rum bottle and we will go meet our friends/" I said.

When we reached the fifth-floor room door, I had JJ ring the bell. When the door started to open, I charged in gun drawn, knocking the secondary chain lock off of the door, and ready for action. I was met by Olivers grizzly stopper pointed at my face and two familiar faces I had seen before, not on a friendly basis behind him with very large revolvers pointed at me. "What the fuck?" I screamed it loud, trying to aim past Oliver's gigantic head to get a bead on the Bobbsey twins. One tooth and no tooth.

"Boys stop it" Susan shouted. "Melvin, I'd like you to meet my cousins, this is Dexter and Bubba." Dexter and Bubba sat on the couch with a case in front of them I had seen before open, to show the 2 million cash we had pitched out the window over the bank which I thought we would never see again.

"Come on in" they said in unison, both with big toothless smiles.

"Ok, what in the fuck is going on? I said at much higher volume than was necessary, waving my fun around pointing it at everyone and no one in particular.

"Boss, you have to calm down, you're going to have a heart attack or a stroke or something. You got to learn to relax, getting all worked up like that is bad for your health." Oliver noted in what I assumed was his most calming tone of voice.

"We have been dodging bullets which are also very bad for my health for the past week." I replied still at a volume that was not required.

"Are you guys' members of the Jackals I said waving the gun at the Bobbsey twins.

"Nah, they just friends of ours. I borrowed a bit of their stationary when they were not looking." One tooth, the one I was thinking the correct name for him was Bubba."

"OK, everyone needs to just calm down," Susan said. Melvin, I understand your confusion so sit and I will explain from the beginning." I had forgotten about Joseph Johnathan Hamilton, still standing in the doorway holding the bottle until he spoke. "Ahh, perhaps everyone could have a drink and calm their nerves." He held up the bottle.

"Excellent idea," no tooth, the one I think was dexter said, I'll get some glasses."

"Sit" Susan instructed turning a chair towards me. I sat as instructed.

"Ok" she started.

"I have explained to you how I ended up married to Dustin Harcourt after a whirlwind romance."

Dexter passed me a glass and Johnathan offered to pour. Just water for mix I'm afraid. He poured me a good shot and I knocked it back. "No water," I said holding the glass for a refill. He filled it and I repeated the emptying process. The next time he filled the glass to the brim.

"So," Susan started again. "As I explained, when the novelty wore off, I was trying to find someplace that I fit where I could be useful. He, and Jessica were very secretive about the business dealings of Harcourt Holdings. I came to suspect two things. One that there was criminal activity involved in the business, and two, that he and Jessica had been lovers long before he met me and still were. When I found out the exorbitant amount of life insurance, he had taken out on himself and me, I wanted out of the relationship. When they found his car over the cliff, Jessica and others tried to convince me he had committed suicide because of me wanting to end the relationship. If they had found his body, I may have agreed with them. It was then I became afraid for myself. It was at this time I became aware of the very large insurance policy on myself as well. That is when I called my cousins whom I knew I could trust. She gestured towards Bubba and Dexter. They convinced me that I would need funds to escape his clutches and that is when we hatched the plan to pay off the Jackals which in reality was just Bubba and Dexter. I was hesitant to trust you as well because Jessica had so highly recommended you. You and Oliver have been great, saved my life several times and I am eternally grateful for that. Obviously, I quickly grew to trust you and wanted to introduce Bubba and Dexter earlier but they thought it may be better, they could be more effective, if they continued to work in the background.

"We had met previously by the way," I interrupted. "Sorry about the tooth Bubba."

"No worries" he fondled the cash in the case on the table. "Made room for some shiny new dentures I will be getting right away"

"So, that was you guys in the 4x4 that collided with the Mercedes knocking it over the cliff? I asked.

"You got it Pontiac. Wrecked the truck pretty good too. Trying to drive it after that, it shook and vibrated so bad, could hardly hold on to the steering wheel. Lasted long enough for us to get back and pick up this though, he patted the case full of money. "That is when we picked up the van. Got a sweetheart of a deal on it."

"So then, let me guess. That was you gentlemen who put the extra bullet hole in the Nissan car that came to Susan's house, and that was you two firing from the hill at the opposite end of the cliff from Oliver, with the automatic weapons, not shooting at us, but shooting at the plane and helicopter? "You got it, caught them fuckers in a crossfire. Teach them to pick on helpless farm girls." He giggled. Susan was obviously far from helpless.

"And, was that your Cadillac when you delivered the burner phone for delivery instructions of the cash?"

"Well, not really ours, Dexter stole that one. He was all worried about his plates being on the 4x4 and getting reported. After that we stole a plate for the 4x4. Easier than stealing the whole vehicle."

My personal phone that I had turned on was vibrating in my pocket. There were several missed calls. I checked the caller id. It said unknown caller. The bad guys had sent a text with threats if I did not answer the call. No texts but I thought I better answer. I slid the screen to connect.

"McCurdy investigations" I answered.

"McCurdy, about time you answered your damn phone." I recognized the voice. It was Sargeant Morgan.

"Good to hear from you to Sargeant Morgan. What can I do for you sir?"

Well, we are out dragging the coast gathering up some body parts. Sharks are having a feast so trying to keep ahead of them. I am sure you know nothing of the aircraft incident from to day, however, Seeing as you still alive, there is not much chance your body parts are among them. Too bad, I was kind of hoping. But seeing as your not among the gory mayhem out here, I thought you may be interested to know who some of the confirmed body pieces belong to. It will take awhile to confirm through DNA testing however, there were a few arms, some with the hands still attached and fingerprints from those pieces indicate they belong to people who homeland security, FBI, CIA, and even Interpol have been hunting for some time now. That fellow your security guard cold cocked still seems to have a failed memory but his fingerprints came back as one of them. It would appear as though there has been a middle eastern cartel, noted for their drugs and human trafficking operating in our fair city. Just to confirm, you would not have any insight into how two aircraft full of very bad foreigners would collide off our coast on a perfectly clear day would you?"

"Well sir, "my cab driver earlier suggested they may have been drinking, but if you suggest there is evidence of drug connections, perhaps they were drunk and stoned. Either that or just unbelievably bad pilots. No wonder they cannot win a war." I replied.

"Yeah McCurdy, you are such a prick. Anyway, as a side note, among the debris floating around we did locate something that may be of interest to that young lady whom I suspect may be your client. A wallet containing the Id of Dustin Harcourt came in from the net. It may have been there since his car took the plunge off the cliff. I expect the rest of him is probably shark shit by now, but I think we could take the ID as an indication he is dead. I leave it to you to break that news to the poor widow. Also among the detritus was a brassiere with one tit in it. DNA will confirm the owner but if you know of any missing women, you might want to put their name forward as a potential victim of todays calamity."

"Thank you, Sargent, the information is sincerely appreciated. I would put forward the name Jessica Baird as a possibility for the deceased tit.

By the way Sargent, we have known each other for a long time and it occurs to me I do not know your first name. I am planning a vacation for myself and my closest friends, someplace tropical course where the rum is excellent, at my expense of course, and I would need a first name to book a first-class ticket to join me."

There was a bit of a pause, then he said, "Dennis" and hung up.

Dennis, I thought WTF? I Never expected that. Hopefully that was my last WTF for today.

It was not to be my last WTF. Not quite.

Susan moved from where she was sitting and sat on Oliver's knee putting her arms around his huge neck and giving him a kiss on the cheek.

Ok, that was a big WTF I never expected.

EPILOGUE

There are beautiful beaches in Mexico, Cuba, and all the Caribbean Islands. Oliver and I had made a pact to visit each of them and do a thorough assessment the climate and the quality of the rum before committing to settling into a new location. Ex marine Jonathan Joseph Hamilton volunteered to assume the additional duties of QA/QC (quality assurance / quality control) for all beverages and was currently enjoying his new duties immensely.

The brassiere Sargent Morgan had fished out of the ocean with a partial teat in it, had been confirmed as belonging to Jessica Baird, which was a shame because it had been a very nice one while it was still attached to her body. Morgan made a special effort to get all of the body the parts sorted for DNA analysis. At least one leg belonged to Dustin Harcourt which would give a good indication to the insurance company that he was no longer among the living. Seeing as Jessica Baird was no longer available to deal with the insurance people, those duties were passed to a reputable legal firm to review. That firm discovered in the fine print, that there was a double indemnity clause for accidental death. The insurance company relented and paid out the funds to Susan. Susan was surprised to learn of this, and grateful as were Oliver and myself when Susan broke the news to us that our commission amount would be based on 20 million, not the agreed upon 10 million.

The feds arrived on the scene to investigate the unusual number of unwelcome foreigners associated with Harcourt holdings. Homeland security, FBI, CIA, ATF, maybe Interpol as well. I am not sure who all they were however as far as I was concerned, they were welcome to the rest of the job.

All the assets of Harcourt holdings were seized temporarily while the investigation was active. Several small properties identified as having illegal activities regards the drug and human trafficking were raided. Some of these were confirmed to be the bases for drug manufacturing and sales. The ATF would become the new owners of these properties. Stragglers of the cartel found in these places were rounded up and either deported immediately or jailed to be deported after serving their sentence. The corporate offices of Harcourt Holdings were returned to Dustin Harcourt's grieving spouse and soul heir.

Answers to my WTF? is going on.

Dustin Harcourt and Jessica Baird were lovers and they had collaborated with the wrong people. In need of funds, Harcourt had become involved with the middle eastern cartel. To the cartel, Harcourt holdings was an opportunity to launder money and gain a foothold in America for their illicit goods and activities. It will never be known whether Dustin and Jessica hatched the plot to collect insurance on their own or with the cartels help. For sure it was a combined effort on Dustin, Jessica and the cartel that was intent on disposing of Susan, and by proxy, myself, and Oliver. Whoever's' s plan it was, it was simple enough. Dustin would marry a girl from some distant hillbilly place, move her to the city, insure her and Dustin's lives exorbitantly with Jessica as executor of the will. On the accidental deaths of Dustin and his spouse, the insurance would revert to the executor of the estate which would be Jessica. With 40 million bucks, Dustin and Jessica could live the rest of their lives in a tropical paradise, and the cartel would have their foothold in America, not only for their illicit activities but also a staging point for the terrorist group they were all a part of. The Jackals had nothing to do with it other than stationary the Bobbsey twins had borrowed. That and an anonymous caller informing them of foreigners cutting into their territory and they needed to be more diligent. I can tolerate home grown criminals.

The errors in their plan were when Dustin married what he thought was a dumb blond farmers daughter whom it turned out was far from dumb, and Jessica sending Susan to a private investigating agency she was certain was the most inept in the city, only to discover that, what this particular agency lacked in smarts was more than made up for by tenacity.

Dumb blond, my ass. Shits and giggles investigations, my ass.

Jonathan Joseph interrupted my reverie, passing me a drink." Try this Boss" he passed me a drink." It is called a Mojito. Made with tequila I think but very tasty." "Thank you, JJ," I said taking a sip. "It is tasty." I made a mental note to check and see if tequila had the same scurvy deterring qualities as rum.

Oliver and the grieving widow Susan were frolicking in the waves on the beach, my new friend Dennis Morgan sat up in the lounge chair beside me, took the mojito offered by JJ.

"Cheers, I raised my glass to him. Salud, he clinked my glass.